Casey Agonistes

Richard Milton McKenna was born in 1913 in Idaho, USA.
He joined the US Navy when he was eighteen and served
for twenty-two years. In 1953 he retired and enrolled in
the University of North Carolina, and started writing full
time in 1958. His most famous work, *The Sand Pebbles*, was
an immediate bestseller when it was published in 1963.
He died in 1964. Of Richard McKenna, Damon Knight writes:
'He was one of the first to realize that science fiction
is not a category but a way of looking at the universe.'

Richard McKenna

CASEY AGONISTES
and other science fiction and fantasy stories

introduction by Damon Knight

Pan Books London and Sydney

'Casey Agonistes' appeared originally in the *Magazine of Fantasy and Science Fiction*, September 1958

'Hunter, Come Home' appeared originally in the *Magazine of Fantasy and Science Fiction*, March 1963

'The Secret Place' appeared originally in *Orbit*, ed. Damon Knight, G. P. Putnam's Sons, 1966

'Mine Own Ways' appeared originally in the *Magazine of Fantasy and Science Fiction*, February 1960

'Fiddler's Green' appeared originally in *Orbit 2*, ed. Damon Knight, G. P. Putnam's Sons, 1967

All of the above stories appear here by permission of Mrs Eva McKenna

First published in Great Britain 1973 by Victor Gollancz Ltd
This edition published 1976 by Pan Books Ltd
Cavaye Place, London SW10 9PG
© the Estate of Richard McKenna, 1973
ISBN 0 330 24825 1
Made and printed in Great Britain by
Hunt Barnard Printing Ltd, Aylesbury, Bucks
This book is sold subject to the condition that it
shall not, by way of trade or otherwise, be lent, re-sold,
hired out or otherwise circulated without the publisher's prior
consent in any form of binding or cover other than that in which
it is published and without a similar condition including this
condition being imposed on the subsequent purchaser

Contents

Introduction 7
Casey Agonistes 11
Hunter, come home 23
The secret place 64
Mine own ways 80
Fiddler's Green 97

Introduction

In photographs taken after he became prosperous you see him wearing well-tailored suits that slim him down, but in his everyday clothes he looked like what he was, a big mick who had worked with his hands all his life. Only when you listened to him talk did you realize that he was a scholar too. His speech was precise, a little diffident, literary – he almost never used slang or obscenity. (In *The Sand Pebbles*, a 597-page novel about American sailors, nobody uses any language stronger than 'God-damn'.)

I first saw his name on a manuscript in 1958 when I was working on the magazine *If*. The previous editor, who was also the publisher, James L. Quinn, had bought the story only after McKenna, at Quinn's request, had cut it from 14,000 words to 7,000. In his essay 'Journey With a Little Man',[1] he describes how he rewrote this story again and again, cutting away paragraphs, then sentences, then individual words. Not many writers would or could have cut that story exactly in half, but McKenna did, and the experience of subjecting every word of it to a merciless criticism taught him something invaluable about writing.

Judith Merril and I invited him to the Milford Science Fiction Writers' Workshop that year; he and his wife, Eva, showed up on the bus, and within two days we were all friends for life. Mac took the Milford workshops with absolute seriousness. He read every story twice, and always found something to praise in it, even if it were only the author's conception which he had not successfully followed. In these workshops and in the correspondence round-robins that some of us organized afterwards, his was the kind of criticism that not only discovered what was

1. *The Sons of Martha and Other Stories* by Richard McKenna, Harper & Row, 1967.

wrong with stories but invented ingenious ways of salvaging them.

Richard Milton McKenna grew up in a town in Idaho not unlike the setting of 'The Secret Place', and there is a touch of autobiography in the character of Owen in that story. The Depression forced him to leave college after a year and join the Navy at eighteen. There, a year or two later, he began trying to educate himself by reading. He found that he couldn't do it; the will to understand was not enough.

In a 1962 speech, 'New Eyes for Old',[2] he compared himself to the caged rats in a Hong Kong bar that were given an egg every night. The starved rats surrounded the egg, struggling in vain to bite through the shell. Somehow they always managed to break the egg and eat it — McKenna never could tell how — it usually took them at least half an hour.

I met books that I could not read. I spent months on some of them. I suspected that the treasure they withheld from me was proportional in richness to the difficulty of getting at it. I would start over again and again, trying to pinpoint the precise page and then paragraph and finally the single word at which my comprehension began to fail. I would squint and scratch my head and chew my pencil. I would writhe my feet and ankles in among the rungs of my chair and sometimes I would grip a book hard enough to tear it . . .

At those times I would be irresistibly reminded of the Hong Kong rats so frantic to break their egg. Once I had laughed at them, and now by some transhuman justice I was in their predicament. No rats were present to laugh at me, so I laughed for them.

To begin with, I had thought a dictionary would be all the help I would need. I did not give up that notion easily. I don't know how many times I looked up the word *ontology* and grasped at it as futilely as the Hong Kong rats would bite at their egg. I used to go into bookstores and look up that word in every dictionary they had, vowing to buy the first one in which I could understand the definition. I never found such a dictionary.

McKenna loved the machinery he worked with, but hated navy life and never felt himself a part of it. He stuck it out for

2. *New Eyes For Old: Nonfiction Writings by Richard McKenna*, John F. Blair, 1972.

twenty-two years, all the same. In 1953 he retired and enrolled in the University of North Carolina to get the education he could not give himself. How much and how well he learned there is abundantly evident in the stories he wrote, some of them published after his death.

'Casey Agonistes' might be described as a study in the psychology of perception, but also, and much more deeply, it concerns itself with ontology – 'the science of being' (*American Heritage Dictionary*): more specifically, the investigation of the nature of reality. In this story McKenna suggests that a recurring hallucination may have as much reality, although of a different sort, as a table or a chair. In 'The Secret Place' and in 'Fiddler's Green', he suggests that the table-and-chair reality is itself an illusion which we ourselves create.

These are not ideas that crop up very often in science fiction, and McKenna, although he conscientiously followed the forms of conventional science fiction, was no ordinary s.f. writer. Once he hit his stride, the trivial puzzles and adventures of science fiction stories were not for him: he tackled the basic problems of philosophy. 'Mine Own Ways', although the first few pages are unfortunately so compressed that they make heavy going, is an exciting attack on the fundamental problem of cultural anthropology: who invented the culture that turned hominids into men? In the process, he explains what ritual ordeals and mutilations are for, and offers a new partial explanation for the celebrated difference between men and women. In 'Hunter, Come Home' he uses similar material in an altogether different way, and yet makes it equally believable.

McKenna's intent from the beginning was to work his way through science fiction into the 'mainstream', because the science fiction audience was limited, and he wanted to reach as many readers as he could. He succeeded a year after his first professional appearance, when the stories that later were integrated into *The Sand Pebbles* began to sell to *The Saturday Evening Post* and elsewhere. Yet he never turned his back on science fiction; he only cast it in a form which he thought would have the greatest popular appeal. *The Sand Pebbles*, he maintained, is science fiction – the science is cultural anthropology. He was one of the first to realize that science fiction is not a category but a way of looking at the universe. More than a decade after these stories were written, they seem more relevant than ever.

Damon Knight

Casey Agonistes

You can't just plain die. You got to do it by the book.

That's how come I'm here in this TB ward with nine other recruits. Basic training to die.

You do it by stages. First a big ward, you walk around and go out and they call you mister. Then, if you got what it takes, a promotion to this isolation ward and they call you charles. You can't go nowhere, you meet the masks, and you get the feel of being dead.

Being dead is being weak and walled off. You hear car noises and see little doll-people down on the sidewalks, but when they come to visit you they wear white masks and nightgowns and talk past you in the wrong voices. They're scared you'll rub some off on them. You would, too, if you knew how.

Nobody ever visits me. I had practice being dead before I come here. Maybe that's how I got to be charles so quick.

It's easy, playing dead here. You eat your pills, make out to sleep in the quiet hours and drink your milk like a good little charles. You grin at their phony joshing about how healthy you look and feel. You all know better, but them's the rules.

Sick call is when they really make you know it. It's a parade — the head doctor and nurse, the floor nurse Mary Howard and two interns, all in masks and nightgowns. Mary pushes the wheeled rack with our fever charts on it. The doc is a tall skinhead with wooden eyes and pinchnose glasses. The head nurse is fat, with little pig eyes and a deep voice.

The doc can't see, hear, smell or touch you. He looks at your reflection in the chart and talks about you like you was real, but it's Mary that pulls down the cover and opens your pyjama coat, and the interns poke and look and listen and tell the doc what they see and hear. He asks them questions for you to answer. You tell them how good you feel and they tell him. He ain't supposed to get contaminated.

Mary's small, dark and sweet and the head nurse gives her a

bad time. One intern is small and dark like Mary, with soft black eyes and very gentle. The other one is pink and chubby.

The doc's voice is high and thin, like he ain't all there below decks. The head nurse snaps at Mary, snips at the interns, and puts a kind of dog wiggle in her voice when she talks to the doc.

I'm glad not to know what's under any of their masks, except maybe Mary's, because I can likely imagine better faces for them than God did. The head nurse makes rounds, writing the book. When she catches us out of line, like smoking or being up in a quiet hour, she gives Mary hell.

She gives us hell too, like we was babies. She kind of hints that if we ain't respectful to her and obey her rules maybe she won't let us die after all.

Christ, how I hate that hag! I hope I meet her in hell.

That's how it struck me, first day or two in isolation. I'd looked around for old shipmates, like a guy does, but didn't see any. On the third day one recognized me. I thought I knew that gravel voice, but even after he told me I couldn't hardly believe it was old Slop Chute Hewitt.

He was skin and bones and his blue eyes had a kind of puzzled look like I saw in them once years ago when a big limey sucker punched him in Nagasaki Joe's. When I remembered that, it made me know, all right.

He said glad to see me there and we both laughed. Some of the others shuffled over in striped bathrobes and all of a sudden I was in like Flynn, knowing Slop Chute. I found out they called the head doc Uncle Death. The fat nurse was Mama Death. The blond intern was Pink Waldo, the dark one Curly Waldo, and Mary was Mary. Knowing things like that is a kind of password.

They said Curly Waldo was sweet on Mary, but he was a poor Italian. Pink Waldo come of good family and was trying to beat him out. They were pulling for Curly Waldo.

When they left, Slop Chute and me talked over old times in China. I kept seeing him like he was on the *John D. Edwards*, sitting with a cup of coffee topside by the after fireroom hatch, while his snipes turned to down below. He wore bleached dungarees and shined shoes and he looked like a lord of the earth. His broad face and big belly. The way he stoked chow into himself in the guinea pullman—that's what give him his name. The way he took aboard beer and samshu in the Kongmoon Happiness Garden. The way he swung the little ne-sans dancing in the hotels on Skibby Hill. Now ... Godalmighty! It made me know.

But he still had the big jack-lantern grin.

'Remember little Connie that danced at the Palais?' he asked.

I remember her, half Portygee, cute as hell.

'You know, Charley, now I'm headed for scrap, the onliest one damn thing I'm sorry for is I didn't shack with her when I had the chance.'

'She was nice,' I said.

'She was green fire in the velvet, Charley. I had her a few times when I was on the *Monocacy*. She wanted to shack and I wouldn't never do it. Christ, Christ, I wish I did, now!'

'I ain't sorry for anything, that I can think of.'

'You'll come to it, sailor. For every guy there's some one thing. Remember how Connie used to put her finger on her nose like a Jap girl?'

'Now, Mr Noble, you mustn't keep arthur awake in quiet hour. Lie down yourself, please.'

It was Mama Death, sneaked up on us.

'Now rest like a good boy, charles, and we'll have you home before you know it,' she told me on her way out.

I thought a thought at her.

*

The ward had green-grey linoleum, high, narrow windows, a spar-colour overhead, and five bunks on a side. My bunk was at one end next to the solarium. Slop Chute was across from me in the middle. Six of us was sailors, three soldiers, and there was one marine.

We got mucho sack time, training for the long sleep. The marine bunked next to me and I saw a lot of him.

He was a strange guy. Name of Carnahan, with a pointed nose and a short upper lip and a go-to-hell stare. He most always wore his radio earphones and he was all the time grinning and chuckling like he was in a private world from the rest of us.

It wasn't the programme that made him grin, either, like I thought first. He'd do it even if some housewife was yapping about how to didify the dumplings. He carried on worst during sick call. Sometimes Uncle Death looked across almost like he could hear it direct.

I asked him about it and he put me off, but finally he told me. Seems he could hypnotize himself to see a big ape and then make the ape clown around. He told me I might could get to see it too. I wanted to try, so we did.

'He's there,' Carnahan would say. 'Sag your eyes, look out the corners. He won't be plain at first.

'Just *expect* him, he'll come. Don't want him to do anything. You just *feel*. He'll do what's natural,' he kept telling me.

I got where I could see the ape — Casey, Carnahan called him — in flashes. Then one day Mama Death was chewing out Mary and I saw him plain. He come up behind Mama and — I busted right out laughing.

He looked like a bowlegged man in an ape suit covered with red-brown hair. He grinned and made faces with a mouth full of big yellow teeth and he was furnished like John Keeno himself. I roared.

'Put on your phones so you'll have an excuse for laughing,' Carnahan whispered. 'Only you and me can see him, you know.'

*

Fixing to be dead, you're ready for God knows what, but Casey was sure something.

'Hell, no, he ain't real,' Carnahan said. 'We ain't so real ourselves any more. That's why we can see him.'

Carnahan told me okay to try and let Slop Chute in on it. It ended we cut the whole gang in, going slow so the masks wouldn't get suspicious.

It bothered Casey at first, us all looking at him. It was like we all had a string on him and he didn't know who to mind. He backed and filled and tacked and yawed all over the ward not able to steer himself. Only when Mama Death was there and Casey went after her, then it was like all the strings pulled the same way.

The more we watched him the plainer and stronger he got till finally he started being his own man. He came and went as he pleased and we never knew what he'd do next except that there'd be a laugh in it. Casey got more and more there for us, but he never made a sound.

He made a big difference. We all wore our earphones and giggled like idiots. Slop Chute wore his big sideways grin more often. Old Webster almost stopped griping.

There was a man filling in for a padre came to visitate us every week. Casey would sit on his knee and wiggle and drool, with one finger between those strong, yellow teeth. The man said the radio was a Godsend to us patient spirits in our hour of trial. He stopped coming.

Casey made a real show out of sick call. He kissed Mama Death smack on her mask, danced with her and bit her on the rump. He rode piggy back on Uncle Death. He even took a hand in Mary's romance.

One Waldo always went in on each side of a bunk to look, listen and feel for Uncle. Mary could go on either side. We kept count of whose side she picked and how close she stood to him. That's how we figured Pink Waldo was ahead.

Well, Casey started to shoo her gently in by Curly Waldo and then crowd her closer to him. And, you know, the count began to change in Curly's favour. Casey had something.

If no masks were around to bedevil, Casey would dance and turn handsprings. He made us all feel good.

Uncle Death smelled a rat and had the radio turned off during sick call and quiet hours. But he couldn't cut off Casey.

*

Something went wrong with Roby, the cheerful black boy next to Slop Chute. The masks were all upset about it and finally Mary come told him on the sly. He wasn't going to make it. They were going to flunk him back to the big ward and maybe back to the world.

Mary's good that way. We never see her face, of course, but I always imagine for her a mouth like Venus has, in that picture you see her standing in the shell.

When Roby had to go, he come around to each bunk and said goodbye. Casey stayed right behind him with his tongue stuck out. Roby kept looking around for Casey, but of course he couldn't see him.

He turned around, just before he left the ward, and all of a sudden Casey was back in the middle and scowling at him. Roby stood looking at Casey with the saddest face I ever saw him wear. Then Casey grinned and waved a hand. Roby grinned back and tears run down his black face. He waved and shoved off.

Casey took to sleeping in Roby's bunk till another recruit come in.

One day two masked orderlies loaded old Webster the whiner on to a go-to-Jesus cart and wheeled him off to X-ray. They said. But later one came back and wouldn't look at us and pushed Webster's locker out and we knew. The masks had him in a quiet room for the graduation exercises.

They always done that, Slop Chute told me, so's not to hurt the morale of the guys not able to make the grade yet. Trouble was, when a guy went to X-ray on a go-to-Jesus cart he never knew till he got back whether he was going to see the gang again.

Next morning when Uncle Death fell in for sick call, Casey come bouncing down the ward and hit him a haymaker plumb on the mask.

I swear the bald-headed bastard staggered. I know his glasses fell off and Pink Waldo caught them. He said something about a moment of vertigo, and made a quick job of sick call. Casey stayed right behind him and kicked his stern post every step he took.

Mary favoured Curly Waldo's side that day without any help from Casey.

*

After that Mama Death really got ugly. She slobbered loving care all over us to keep us from knowing what we was there for. We got baths and back rubs we didn't want. Quiet hour had to start on the dot and be really quiet. She was always reading Mary off in whispers, like she knew it bothered us.

Casey followed her around aping her duck waddle and poking her behind now and again. We laughed and she thought it was at her and I guess it was. So she got Uncle Death to order the routine temperatures taken rectally, which she knew we hated. We stopped laughing and she knocked off the rectal temperatures. It was a kind of unspoken agreement. Casey give her a worse time than ever, but we saved our laughing till she was gone.

Poor Slop Chute couldn't do anything about his big, lopsided grin that was louder than a belly laugh. Mama give him a real bad time. She arthured the hell out of him.

He was coming along first rate, had another haemorrhage, and they started taking him to the clinic on a go-to-Jesus cart instead of in a chair. He was supposed to use ducks and a bedpan instead of going to the head, but he saved it up and after lights out we used to help him walk to the head. That made his reflection in the chart wrong and got him in deeper with Uncle Death.

I talked to him a lot, mostly about Connie. He said he dreamed about her pretty often now.

'I figure it means I'm near ready for the deep six, Charley.'

'Figure you'll see Connie then?'

'No. Just hope I won't have to go on thinking about her then. I want it to be all night in and no reveille.'

'Yeah,' I said, 'me too. What ever become of Connie?'

'I heard she ate poison right after the Reds took over Shanghai. I wonder if she ever dreamed about me?'

'I bet she did, Slop Chute,' I said. 'She likely used to wake up screaming and she ate the poison just to get rid of you.'

He put on his big grin.

'You regret something too, Charley. You find it yet?'

'Well, maybe,' I said. 'Once on a stormy night at sea on the *Black Hawk* I had a chance to push King Brody over the side. I'm sorry now I didn't.'

'Just come to you?'

'Hell, no, it come to me three days later when he give me a week's restriction in Tsingtao. I been sorry ever since.'

'No. It'll smell you out, Charley. You wait.'

Casey was shadow boxing down the middle of the ward as I shuffled back to my bunk.

*

It must've been spring because the days were longer. One night, right after the nurse come through, Casey and Carnahan and me helped Slop Chute walk to the head. While he was there he had another haemorrhage.

Carnahan started for help but Casey got in the way and motioned him back and we knew Slop Chute didn't want it.

We pulled Slop Chute's pyjama top off and steadied him. He went on his knees in front of the bowl and the soft, bubbling cough went on for a long time. We kept flushing it. Casey opened the door and went out to keep away the nurse.

Finally it pretty well stopped. Slop Chute was too weak to stand. We cleaned him up and I put my pyjama top on him, and we stood him up. If Casey hadn't took half the load, we'd'a never got him back to his bunk.

Godalmighty! I used to carry hundred-kilo sacks of cement like they was nothing.

We went back and cleaned up the head. I washed out the pyjama top and draped it on the radiator. I was in a cold sweat and my face burned when I turned in.

Across the ward Casey was sitting like a statue beside Slop Chute's bunk.

Next day was Friday, because Pink Waldo made some crack about fish to Curly Waldo when they formed up for sick call. Mary moved closer to Curly Waldo and gave Pink Waldo a cold look. That was good.

Slop Chute looked waxy, and Uncle Death seemed to see it because a gleam come into his wooden eyes. Both Waldos listened all over Slop Chute and told uncle what they heard in their secret language. Uncle nodded, and Casey thumbed his nose at him.

No doubt about it, the ways was greased for Slop Chute. Mama Death come back soon as she could and began to loosen the chocks. She slobbered arthurs all over Slop Chute and flittered around like women do when they smell a wedding. Casey give her extra special hell, and we all laughed right out and she hardly noticed.

That afternoon two orderly-masks come with a go-to-Jesus cart and wanted to take Slop Chute to X-ray. Casey climbed on the cart and scowled at them.

Slop Chute told 'em shove off, he wasn't going.

They got Mary and she told Slop Chute please go, it was doctor's orders.

'Sorry, no,' he said.

'Please, for me, Slop Chute,' she begged.

She knows our right names – that's one reason we love her. But Slop Chute shook his head, and his big jaw bone stuck out.

Mary – she had to then – called Mama Death. Mama waddled in, and Casey spit in her mask.

'Now, arthur, what is this, arthur, you know we want to help you get well and go home, arthur,' she arthured at Slop Chute. 'Be a good boy now, arthur, and go along to the clinic.'

She motioned the orderlies to pick him up anyway. Casey hit one in the mask and Slop Chute growled, 'Sheer off, you bastards!'

The orderlies hesitated.

Mama's little eyes squinted and she wiggled her hands at them. 'Let's not be naughty, arthur. Doctor knows best, arthur.'

The orderlies looked at Slop Chute and at each other. Casey wrapped his arms and legs around Mama Death and began chewing on her neck. He seemed to mix right into her, someway, and she broke and run out of the ward.

She come right back, though, trailing Uncle Death. Casey met him at the door and beat hell out of him all the way to Slop Chute's bunk. Mama sent Mary for the chart, and Uncle Death studied Slop Chute's reflection for a minute. He looked pale and swayed a little from Casey's beating.

He turned toward Slop Chute and breathed in deep and Casey was on him again. Casey wrapped his arms and legs around him and chewed at his mask with those big yellow teeth. Casey's hair bristled and his eyes were red as the flames of hell.

Uncle Death staggered back across the ward and fetched up against Carnahan's bunk. The other masks were scared spitless, looking all around, kind of knowing.

Casey pulled away, and Uncle Death said maybe he was wrong, schedule it for tomorrow. All the masks left in a hurry except Mary. She went back to Slop Chute and took his hand.

'I'm sorry, Slop Chute,' she whispered.

'Bless you, Connie,' he said, and grinned. It was the last thing I ever heard him say.

*

Slop Chute went to sleep and Casey sat beside his bunk. He

motioned me off when I wanted to help Slop Chute to the head after lights out. I turned in and went to sleep.

I don't know what woke me. Casey was moving around fidgety-like, but of course not making a sound. I could hear the others stirring and whispering in the dark too.

Then I heard a muffled noise – the bubbling cough again, and spitting. Slop Chute was having another haemorrhage and he had his head under the blankets to hide the sound. Carnahan started to get up. Casey waved him down.

I saw a deeper shadow high in the dark over Slop Chute's bunk. It came down ever so gently and Casey would push it back up again. The muffled coughing went on.

Casey had a harder time pushing back the shadow. Finally he climbed on the bunk straddle of Slop Chute and kept a steady push against it.

The blackness came down anyway, little by little. Casey strained and shifted his footing. I could hear him grunt and hear his joints crack.

I was breathing forced draught with my heart like to pull off its bed bolts. I heard other bedsprings creaking. Somebody across from me whimpered low, but it was sure never Slop Chute that done it.

Casey went to his knees, his hands forced almost level with his head. He swung his head back and forth and I saw his lips curled back from the big teeth clenched tight together ... Then he had the blackness on his shoulders like the weight of the whole world.

Casey went down on hands and knees with his back arched like a bridge. Almost I thought I heard him grunt ... and he gained a little.

Then the blackness settled heavier, and I heard Casey's tendons pull out and his bones snap. Casey and Slop Chute disappeared under the blackness, and it overflowed from there over the whole bed ... and more ... and it seemed to fill the whole ward.

It wasn't like going to sleep, but I don't know anything it was like.

*

The masks must've towed off Slop Chute's hulk in the night, because it was gone when I woke up.

So was Casey.

Casey didn't show up for sick call and I knew then how much he meant to me. With him around to fight back I didn't feel as dead as they wanted me to. Without him I felt deader than ever. I even almost liked Mama Death when she charlesed me.

Mary came on duty that morning with a diamond on her third finger and a brighter sparkle in her eye. It was a little diamond, but it was Curly Waldo's and it kind of made up for Slop Chute.

I wished Casey was there to see it. He would've danced all around her and kissed her nice, the way he often did. Casey loved Mary.

It was Saturday, I know, because Mama Death come in and told some of us we could be wheeled to a special church hooraw before breakfast next morning if we wanted. We said no thanks. But it was a hell of a Saturday without Casey. Sharkey Brown said it for all of us – 'With Casey gone, this place is like a morgue again.'

Not even Carnahan could call him up.

'Sometimes I think I feel him stir, and then again I ain't sure,' he said. 'It beats hell where he's went to.'

Going to sleep that night was as much like dying as it could be for men already dead.

*

Music from far off woke me up when it was just getting light. I was going to try to cork off again, when I saw Carnahan was awake.

'Casey's around somewhere,' he whispered.

'Where?' I asked, looking around. 'I don't see him.'

'I feel him,' Carnahan said. 'He's around.'

The others began to wake up and look around. It was like the night Casey and Slop Chute went under. Then something moved in the solarium...

It was Casey.

He come in the ward slow and bashful-like, jerking his head

all around, with his eyes open wide, and looking scared we was going to throw something at him. He stopped in the middle of the ward.

'Yea, Casey!' Carnahan said in a low, clear voice.

Casey looked at him sharp.

'Yea, Casey!' we all said. 'Come aboard, you hairy old bastard!'

Casey shook hands with himself over his head and went into his dance. He grinned ... and I swear to God it was Slop Chute's big, lopsided grin he had on.

For the first time in my whole damn life I wanted to cry.

Hunter, come home

On that planet the damned trees were immortal, the new guys said in disgust, so there was no wood for camp fires and they had to burn pyrolene doused on raw stem fragments. Roy Craig crouched over the fire tending a bubbling venison stew and caught himself wishing they might still use the electric galley inside their flyer. But these new guys were all red dots and they wanted flame in the open and they were right, of course.

Four of them sat across the fire from Craig, talking loudly and loading explosive pellets. They wore blue field denims and had roached hair and a red dot tattooed on their foreheads. Bork Wilde, the new field chief, stood watching them. He was tall and bold-featured, with roached black hair, and he had two red dots on his forehead. Craig's reddish hair was unroached and, except for freckles, his forehead was blank, because he had never taken the Mordin manhood test. For all his gangling young six-foot body, he felt like a boy among men. Under the new deal he caught all the menial camp jobs, and he didn't like it.

They were a six-man ringwalling crew and they were camped beside their flyer, a grey, high-sided cargo job, a safe two miles downslope from the big ringwall. All around them the bare, fluted, silvery stems speared and branched fifty feet overhead and gave a watery cast to the twilight. Normally the stems would be covered with two-lobed phytozoon leaves of all sizes and colour patterns. The men and their fire had excited the leaves and they had detached themselves, to hover in a pulsating rainbow cloud high enough to catch the sun above the silver tracery of the upper branches. They piped and twittered and shed a spicy perfume, and certain daring ones dipped low above the men. One of the pellet loaders, a rat-faced little man named Cobb, hurled a flaming chunk up through them.

'Shut up, you stupid flitterbugs!' he roared. 'Let a man hear himself think!'

The men laughed. The red-and-white fibrous root tangle

underfoot was slowly withdrawing, underground and to the sides, leaving bare soil around the fire. The new guys thought it was to escape the fire, but Craig remembered the roots had always done that when the old ringwall crew used to camp without fire. By morning the whole area around the flyer would be bare soil. A brown, many-legged crawler an inch long pushed out of the exposed soil and scuttled after the retreating roots. Craig smiled and stirred the stew. A small green-and-red phyto leaf dropped from the cloud and settled on his knobby wrist. He let it nuzzle at him. Its thin, velvety wings waved slowly. A much thickened midrib made a kind of body with no head or visible appendages. Craig turned his wrist over and wondered idly why the phyto didn't fall off. Then a patterned green-and-gold phyto with wings large as dinner plates settled on Wilde's shoulder. Wilde snatched it and tore its wings with thick fingers. It whimpered and fluttered. Distress shadowed Craig's gaunt, sensitive face.

'It can't hurt you, Mr Wilde,' he protested. 'It's just curious.'

'Who pulled your trigger, Blanky?' Wilde snapped. 'I wish these damn bloodsucking butterflies *could* know what I'm doing here!'

He turned and kicked one of the weak, turgor-rigid stems and brought it crumpling down across the flyer. He threw the torn phyto after it and laughed, showing big horse teeth. Craig bit his lip.

'Chow's ready,' he said. 'Come and get it.'

*

After cleanup it got dark, with only one moon in the sky, and the phytos furled their wings and went to sleep on the upper branches. The fire died away and the men rolled up in blankets and snored. Craig sat up, not able to sleep. He saw Sidis come and stand looking out the lighted doorway of the flyer's main cabin. Sidis was a Belconti ecologist who had been boss of the old ringwall crew and he was along on this trip just to break Wilde in as his replacement. He insisted on eating and sleeping inside the flyer, to the scorn of the Planet Mordin red dots. His forehead was blank as Craig's, but that was little comfort. Sidis was from Planet Belconti, where they had different customs.

For Mordinmen, courage was the supreme good. They were descendants of a lost Earth-colony that had lapsed to a stone-age technology and fought its way back to gunpowder in ceaseless war against the fearsome Great Russel dinotheres that were the dominant life-form on Planet Mordin before men came. For many generations young candidates for manhood went forth in a sworn band to kill a Great Russel with spears and arrows. When rifles came, they hunted him singly. Survivors wore the red dot of manhood and fathered the next generation. Then the civilized planets discovered Mordin, knowledge flowed in, and population exploded. Suddenly there were too few Great Russels left to meet the need. Craig's family had not been able to buy him a Great Russel hunt.

I'll kill one, when I get my chance, Craig thought. Mr Wilde killed two. That don't seem fair.

Ten years before Craig's birth, the Mordin Hunt Council found the phyto planet unclaimed and set out to convert it to one great dinothere hunting range. The Earth-type Mordin biota could neither eat nor displace the alien phytos. Mordin contracted with Belconti biologists to exterminate the native life. Mordin labourers served under Belconti biotechs. All were blankies; no red dots would serve under the effete Belcontis, many of whom were women. Using the killer plant *Thanasis*, the Belcontis cleared two large islands and restocked them with a Mordin biota. They made a permanent base on one of the islands and attacked the three continents.

When I was little, they told me I'd kill my Great Russel on this planet, Craig thought. He clasped his arms around his knees. There was still only one Great Russel on the planet, on one of the cleared islands.

Because for thirty years the continents refused to die. The phytos encysted *Thanasis* areas, adapted, recovered ground. Belconti genesmiths designed ever more deadly strains of *Thanasis*, pushing it to the safe upper limit of its recombination index, and it began losing ground. The Belcontis said the attempt must be given up. But the planet had become a symbol of future hope to curb present social unrest on Mordin and the Hunt Council refused to give up. It sent red dots to study biotechnics on Belconti.

Craig had come to the planet on a two-year labour contract. He had enjoyed working with other blankies under a Belconti boss and he had almost forgotten the pain of withheld manhood. He had extended his contract for another two years. Then the Mordin relief ship a month ago landed a full crew of red dots, including biotechs to replace the Belcontis, who were all to go home in about a year, when their own relief ship came. Craig was left the only blanky on the planet, except for the Belcontis, and they didn't count.

I'm already alone, he thought. He bowed his head on his knees and wished he could sleep. Someone touched his shoulder and he looked up to see Sidis beside him.

'Come inside, will you, Roy?' he whispered. 'I want to talk to you.'

*

Craig sat down across from Sidis at the long table in the main cabin. Sidis was a slender, dark man with gentle Belconti manners and a wry smile.

'I'm worried about you for these next two years,' he said. 'I don't like the way they order you around, that nasty little fellow Cobb in particular. Why do you take it?'

'I have to because I'm a blanky,' Craig said.

'You can't help that. If it's one of your laws, it's unfair.'

'It's fair because it's natural,' Craig said. 'I don't like not being a man, but that's just the way things are with me.'

'You are a man. You're twenty-four years old.'

'I'm not a man until I feel like one,' Craig said. 'I can't feel like one until I kill my Great Russel.'

'I'm afraid you'd still feel out of place,' Sidis said. 'I've watched you for two years and I think you have a certain quality your own planet has no use for. So I have a proposition for you.' He glanced at the door, then back to Craig. 'Declare yourself a Belconti citizen, Roy. We'll all sponsor you and I know Mil Ames will find you a job on the staff. You can go home to Belconti with us.'

'Great Russel!' Craig said. 'I could never do that, Mr Sidis.'

'How is life on Mordin for a blanky? Could he get a wife?'

'Maybe. She'd be some woman that's gave up hope of being even number three wife to a red dot.' Craig frowned and thought about his own father. 'She'd hate him all her life for her bad luck.'

'And you call that fair?'

'It's fair because it's natural. It's natural for a woman to want an all-the-way man instead of a boy that just grew up.'

'Not Belconti women. How about it, Roy?'

Craig clasped his hands between his knees. He lowered his head and shook it slowly.

'No. No, I couldn't. My place is here, fighting for a time when no kid has to grow up cheated, like I been.' He raised his head. 'Besides, no Mordinman ever runs away from a fight.'

Sidis smiled gently. 'This fight is already lost,' he said.

'Not the way Mr Wilde talks,' Craig said. 'Back in the labs at Base Camp they're going to use a trans-something, I hear.'

'Translocator in the gene matrix,' Sidis said. 'I guarantee they won't do it while Mil Ames runs the labs. After we go, they'll probably kill themselves in a year.' He looked doubtfully at Craig. 'I hadn't meant to tell you that, but it's one reason I hope you'll leave with us.'

'How kill ourselves?'

'With an outlaw free-system.'

Craig shook his head and Sidis smiled.

'Look, you know how the phyto stems are all rooted together underground like one big plant,' he said. 'You know we design the self-duplicating enzyme systems that *Thanasis* pumps into them. You know *Thanasis* free-systems can digest a man, too, and that's what you get inoculated against each time we design a new one. Well then.' He steepled his fingers. 'With translocation, *Thanasis* can redesign its own free-systems in the field, in a way. It might come up with something impossible to immunize. It might change so that our specific control virus would no longer kill it. Then it would kill us and rule the planet itself.'

'I don't get all that,' Craig said.

'Then trust my word. It happened once, on Planet Froy.'

Craig nodded. 'I heard about Planet Froy.'

'That's what you risk and you can't win anyway. So come to Planet Belconti with us.'

Craig stood up. 'I almost wish you didn't tell me that,' he said. 'Now I can't even think about leaving.'

Sidis leaned back and spread his fingers on the table.

'Talk to Midori Blake before you say no,' he said. 'I know she's fond of you, Roy. I thought you rather liked her.'

Craig felt his face burn. 'I do like to be around her,' he said. 'I liked it when you used to stop at Burton Island instead of camping in the field. I wish Mr Wilde would go there.'

'I'll try to persuade him. Think it over, will you?'

'I can't think,' Craig said. 'I don't know what I feel.' He turned to the door. 'I'm going out and walk and try to think.'

'Good night, Roy.' Sidis reached for a book.

*

The second moon was just rising. Craig walked through a jungle of ghostly silver stems. Phytos clinging to them piped sleepily, disturbed by his passage. 'I'm too ignorant to be a Belconti,' he said once, aloud. He neared the ringwall. Stems grew more thickly, became harder, fused at last into a sloping ninety-foot dam. Craig climbed halfway up and stopped. It was foolhardy to go higher without a protective suit. *Thanasis* was on the other side, and its free-systems diffused hundreds of feet even in still air. The phyto stems were all rooted together into one big plant and *Thanasis* ate into it like a sickness. The stems formed ringwalls around stands of *Thanasis*, to stop its spread. Craig climbed a few feet higher.

Sure I'm big enough to whip Cobb, he thought. Whip any of them, except Mr Wilde. But he knew in a quarrel his knees would turn to water and his voice squeak off to nothing, because they were men and he was not. 'I'm not a coward,' he said aloud. 'I'll kill my Great Russel yet.'

He climbed to the top. *Thanasis* stretched off in a sea of blackness beneath the moons. Just below he could see the outline of narrow leaves furred with stinging hairs and beaded with poison droplets meant to be rainwashed into the roots of downslope prey. The ringwall impounded the poisoned water and this stand of *Thanasis* was drowning in it and it was desperate. He saw the tendrils, hungry to release poison into enemy tissues and follow after to suck and absorb. (They felt his warmth and waved feebly.) This below him was the woody, climbing form, but they said even waist-high shrubs could eat a man in a week.

I'm not afraid, Craig thought. He sat down and took off his boots and let his bare feet dangle above the *Thanasis*. Midori Blake and all the Belcontis would think this was crazy. They didn't understand about courage — all they had was brains. He liked them anyway, Midori most of all. He thought about her as he gazed off across the dark *Thanasis*. The whole continent would have to be like that first. Then they'd kill off *Thanasis* with a control virus and plant grass and real trees and it would all be like Base and Russel Islands were now. Sidis was wrong — that trans-stuff would do it. He'd stay and help. He felt better, with his mind made up.

Then he felt a gentle tug at his left ankle. It stabbed with fierce and sudden pain. He jerked his leg up. The tendril broke and came with it, still squirming and stinging. Craig whistled and swore as he scraped it off with a boot heel, careful not to let it touch his hands. Then he pulled on his right boot and hurried back to camp for treatment. He carried his left boot, because he knew how fast his ankle would swell. He reached camp with his left leg one screaming ache. Sidis was still up. He neutralized the poison, gave Craig a sedative, and made him take one of the bunks inside the flyer. He didn't ask question just looked down at Craig with his wry smile.

'You Mordinmen,' he said, and shook his head.

The Belcontis were always saying that.

In the morning Cobb sneered and Wilde was furious.

'If you're shooting for a week on the sick list, aim again,' Wilde said. 'I'll give you two days.'

'I'll do his work,' Sidis said. 'He needs two weeks to recover.'

'I'll work,' Craig said. 'It don't hurt so much I can't work.'

'Take today off,' Wilde said, mollified.

'I'll work today,' Craig said. 'I'm all right.'

It was a tortured day under the hot yellow sun, with his foot wrapped in sacks and stabbing pain up his spine with every step. Craig drove his power auger deep into basal ringwall tissue and the aromatic, red-purple sap gushed out and soaked his feet. Then he pushed in the explosive pellet, shouldered his rig and paced off the next position. Over and over he did it, like a machine, not stopping to eat his lunch, ignoring the phytos that clung to his neck and hands. He meant to finish his arc first if it killed him. But when he finished and had time to think about it, his foot felt better than it had all day. He snapped a red cloth to his auger shaft and waved it high and the flyer slanted down to pick him up. Sidis was at the controls.

'You're the first to finish,' he said. 'I don't see why you're even alive. Go and lie down now.'

'I'll take the controls,' Craig said. 'I feel good.'

Sidis shrugged. 'I guess you're proving something,' he said.

He gave Craig the controls and went aft. Driving the flyer was one of the menial jobs that Craig liked. He liked being alone in the little control cabin, with its two seats and windows all around. He lifted to a thousand feet and glanced along the ringwall, curving out of sight in both directions. The pent sea of *Thanasis* was dark green by daylight. The phyto area outside the ringwall gleamed silvery, with an overplay of shifting colours, and it was very beautiful. Far and high in the north he saw a coloured cloud among the fleecy ones. It was a mass of migratory phytos drifting in the wind with their hydrogen sacs inflated. It was beautiful, too.

'They transfer substance to grow the ringwalls,' he heard Sidis telling Wilde back in the main cabin. 'You'll notice the biomass downslope is less dense. When you release that poisoned water from inside the ringwall, you get a shock effect and *Thanasis* follows up fast. But a new ringwall always forms.'

'Next time through I'll blow fifty-mile arcs,' Wilde said.

Craig slanted down to pick up Jordan. He was a stocky, sandy-haired man about Craig's age. He scrambled aboard grinning.

'Beat us again, hey, Craig?' he said. 'That took guts, boy. You're all right!'

'I got two years' practice on you guys,' Craig said.

The praise made him feel good. It was the first time Jordan had called him by name instead of 'Blanky'. He lifted the flyer again. Jordan sat down in the spare seat.

'How's the foot?' he asked.

'Pretty good. I think I could get my boot on, unlaced,' Craig said.

'I'll take camp chores tonight,' Jordan said. 'You rest that foot, Craig. You're too good a man to lose.'

'There's Whelan's flag,' Craig said.

He felt himself blushing with pleasure as he slanted down to pick up Whelan. Jordan went aft. When Rice and Cobb had been picked up, Craig hovered the flyer at two miles and Wilde pulsed off the explosive. Twenty miles of living ringwall tissue fountained in dust and flame. Phytos rising in terrified, chromatic clouds marked the rolling shock wave. Behind it the silvery plain darkened with the sheet flow of poisoned water.

'Hah! Go it, *Thanasis*!' Wilde shouted. 'I swear to bullets, that's a pretty sight down there! Now where's a safe place to camp, Sidis?'

'We're only an hour from Burton Island,' Sidis said. 'I used to stop at the taxonomy station there every night, when we worked this area.'

'Probably why you never got anywhere, too,' Wilde said. 'But I want a look at that island. The Huntsman's got plans for it.'

He shouted orders up to Craig. Craig lifted to ten miles and headed southeast at full throttle. A purplish sea rolled above the silvery horizon. Far on the sea rim beaded islands climbed to view. It had been a good day, Craig thought. Jordan seemed to want to be friends. And now, at last, he'd see Midori Blake again.

He grounded the flyer on slagged earth near the familiar grey stone buildings on the eastern headland. The men got out and George and Helen Toyama, smiling and grey-haired in lab smocks, came to welcome them. Craig's left boot was tight and it hurt, but he could wear it unlaced. Helen told him Midori was painting in the gorge. He limped down the gorge path, past Midori's small house and the Toyama home on the cliff edge at left. Midori and the Toyamas were the only people on Burton Island. The island was a phyto research sanctuary and had never been touched by *Thanasis*. It was the only place other than Base Camp where humans lived permanently.

The gorge was Midori's special place. She painted it over and over, never satisfied. Craig knew it well, the quartz ledge, the cascading waterfall and pool, the phytos dancing in sunlight that the silvery stem forest changed to the quality of strong moonlight. Craig liked watching Midori paint, most of all when she forgot him and sang to herself. She was clean and apart and never resentful or demanding, and it was just good to be in the same world with her. Through the plash of the waterfall and the phyto piping Craig heard her singing before he came upon her, standing before her easel beside a quartz boulder. She heard him and turned and smiled warmly.

'Roy! I'm so glad to see you,' she said. 'I was afraid you'd gone home after all.'

She was small and dainty under her grey dress, with large black eyes and delicate features. Her dark hair snugged boyishly close to her head. Her voice had a natural, birdlike quality, and she moved and gestured with the quick grace of a singing bird. Craig grinned happily.

'For a while I almost wished I did,' he said. 'Now I'm glad again I didn't.' He limped towards her.

'Your foot!' she said. 'Come over here and sit down.' She tugged him to a seat on the boulder. 'What happened?'

'Touch of *Thanasis*,' he said. 'Nothing much.'

'Take off your boot! You don't want pressure on it.'

She helped him take the boot off and ran cool fingertips lightly over the red, swollen ankle. Then she sat beside him.

'I know it hurts you. How did it happen?'

'I was kind of unhappy,' he said. 'I went and sat on a ringwall and let my bare feet hang over.'

'Foolish Roy. Why were you unhappy?'

'Oh – things.' Several brilliant phytos settled on his bared ankle. He let them stay. 'We got to sleep in the field now, 'stead of coming here. The new boss thinks our old gang was lazy. The new guys are all red dots and I'm just a nothing again and – oh, hell!'

'You mean they think they're better than you?'

'They are better, and that's what hurts. Killing a Great Russel is a kind of spirit thing, Midori.' He scuffed his right foot. 'I'll see the day when this planet has enough Great Russels so no kid has to grow up cheated, like I been.'

'The phytos are not going to die, Roy,' she said softly. 'It's very clear now. We're defeated.'

'You Belcontis are. Mordinmen never give up.'

'*Thanasis* is defeated. Will you shoot phytos with rifles?'

'Please don't joke about rifles,' he said. 'We're going to use a trans-something on *Thanasis*.'

'Translocation? Oh no! It can't be controlled for field use. They wouldn't dare!'

'Red dots dare anything,' he said proudly. 'These guys all studied on Belconti; they know how. That's another thing—'

He scuffed his foot again. Phytos were on both their heads and shoulders now and all over his bared ankle. They twittered faintly.

'What, Roy?'

'I feel like an ignorant nothing. Here I been ringwalling for two years, and they already know more about phytos than I do. I want you to tell me something about phytos that I can use to make the guys notice me. Like, can phytos feel?'

She held her hand to her cheek, silent a moment.

'Phytos are strange and wonderful and I love them,' she said softly. 'They're mixed plant and animal. Life never split itself apart on this planet.'

The flying phytozoons, she explained, functioned as leaves for the vegetative stems. But the stems, too, had internal temperature control. The continental networks of great conduit roots moved fluids with a reversible, valved peristalsis. A stem plus attached phytos made an organism.

'But any phyto, Roy, can live with any stem, and they're forever shifting. Everything is part of everything,' she said. 'Our job here on Burton Island is to classify the phytos, and we just can't do it. They vary continuously along every dimension we choose, physical or chemical, and *kind* simply has no meaning.' She sighed. 'That's the most wonderful thing I know about them. Will that help you?'

'I don't get all that. That's what I mean, I'm ignorant,' he said. 'Tell me some one simple thing I can use to make the guys take notice of me.'

'All right, tell them this,' she said. 'Phyto colour patterns are plastid systems that synthesize different molecules. The way they can recombine parts to form new organisms gives them a humanly inconceivable biochemical range. Whatever new poison or free-system we design for *Thanasis*, somewhere by sheer chance they hit on a countersubstance. The knowledge spreads faster each time. That's why *Thanasis* is defeated.'

'I couldn't say that, and don't you say it either, Midori,' Craig protested. 'This here translocation, now—'

'Not even that.' Her voice was faintly sharp. 'The phytos have unlimited translocation and any number of sexes. Collectively, I don't doubt they're the mightiest biochemical lab in the galaxy. They form a kind of biochemical intelligence, almost a mind, and it's learning faster than we are.' She turned and shook his arm with both her small hands. 'Yes, tell them, make them understand,' she said. 'Human intelligence is defeated here. Now human ferocity—oh, Roy—'

'Say it,' he said bitterly. 'Mordinmen are stupid. I ought to know. You sound almost like you want us to lose, Midori.'

She turned away and began cleaning her brushes. It was nearly dark and the phytos were going to rest on the stems overhead. Craig sat miserably silent, remembering the feel of her hands on his arm. Then she spoke, and her voice was soft again.

'I don't know. If you wanted homes and farms here—but you want only the ritual deaths of man and dinothere—'

'You Belcontis can't understand,' Craig said. 'Maybe people's souls get put together different ways on different planets. I know there's a piece missing out of mine and I know what it is.' He put his hand lightly on her shoulder. 'Some holidays I fly down to Russel Island just to look at the Great Russel there, and then I know. I wish I could take you to see him; he'd make you understand.'

'I understand. I just don't agree.'

She swished and splashed brushes, but she didn't pull her shoulder away from his hand. Craig wished he dared ask her about the phytos and that many-sex stuff; the guys'd like that. He blushed and shook his head.

'Why is it you never see a dead phyto? Why is it there ain't enough dead wood on a whole continent to make one camp fire?' he asked. 'What eats 'em? What keeps 'em down?'

She laughed and turned back to him, making his arm slide across her shoulders. He barely let it touch her, and she seemed not to know.

'They eat themselves internally, resorption, we call it,' she said. 'They can grow themselves again in another place and form, as a ringwall, for instance. Roy, this planet has never known death and decay. Everything is resorbed and reconstituted. We try to kill it and it suffers, but its—' her voice trembled—'yes, its *mind*—can't form the idea of death. There's no way to think death biochemically.'

'Oh bullets, Midori! Phytos can't think,' he said. 'I wonder, can they even feel?'

She jumped up and away from his arm. 'Yes, they feel! Their piping is a cry of pain,' she said. 'Papa Toyama can remember when the planet was almost silent. Since he's been here, twenty years, their temperature has risen twelve degrees, their metabolic rate and speed of neural impulse doubled, chronaxy halved—'

Craig stood up too and raised his hands.

'Hold your fire, Midori,' he said. 'You know I don't know all them words. You're mad at me.' It was too dark to see her face plainly.

'I think I'm just terribly afraid,' she said. 'I'm afraid of what we've been doing that we don't know about.'

'That piping has always made me feel sad, kind of,' Craig said. 'I never would hurt a phyto. But Great Russel, when you think about whole continents hurting and crying, day and night for years—you scare me too, Midori.'

She began packing her painting kit. Craig pulled on his boot. It laced up easily. I ain't really scared, he thought.

'We'll go to my house and I'll make our supper,' she said.

She didn't sound angry. He took the kit and walked beside her, hardly limping at all. They started up the cliff path.

'Why did you stay on here, if the work makes you sad?' she asked.

'Two more years and I'll have enough saved to buy me a Great Russel hunt,' he said. He flushed and was glad it was dark. 'I guess you think that's a pretty silly reason.'

'Not at all. I thought you might have an even sillier one.'

He fumbled for a remark, trying not to understand her sudden chill. Then Jordan's voice bawled from above.

'Craig! Ho Craig!'

'Craig aye!'

'Come arunning!' Jordan yelled. 'Bork's raising hell cause you ain't loading pellets. I saved chow for you.'

*

The rest of the field job was much better. Jordan helped on camp chores and joked Rice and Whelan into following suit. Only Wilde and Cobb still called Craig 'Blanky'. Craig felt good about things. Jordan sat beside him in the control cabin as Craig brought the flyer home to Base Island. Russel Island loomed blue to the south and the Main Continent coast range toothed the eastern sea rim.

'Home again. Beer and the range, eh, Craig?' Jordan said. 'We'll get in some hunting, maybe.'

'Hope so,' Craig said.

Base Island looked good. It was four thousand square miles of savanna and rolling hills with stands of young oak and beech. It teemed with game birds and animals transplanted from Mordin. On its northern tip, buildings and fields made the rectilinear pattern of man. Sunlight gleamed on square miles of *Thanasis* greenhouses behind their ionic stockades. Base Island was a promise of the planet's future, when *Thanasis* would have killed off the phytos and been killed in its turn and the wholesome life of Planet Mordin replaced them both. Base Island was home.

They were the first ringwalling team to come in. Wilde reported twelve hundred miles of ringwall destroyed, fifty per cent better than the old Belconti average. Barim, the Chief Huntsman, congratulated them. He was a burly, deep-voiced man with roached grey hair and four red dots on his forehead. It was the first time Craig had ever shaken hands with a man who had killed four Great Russels. Barim rewarded the crew with a week on food-hunting detail. Jordan teamed up with Craig. Craig shot twenty deer and twelve pigs and scores of game birds. His bag was better than Cobb's. Jordan joked at Cobb about it, and it made the sparrowy little man very angry.

The new men had brought a roaring, jovial atmosphere to Base Camp that Craig rather liked. He picked up camp gossip. Barim had ordered immediate production of translocator pollen. Mildred Ames, the Belconti Chief Biologist, had refused. But the labs and equipment were Mordin property and Barim had ordered his own men to go to work on it. Miss Ames raised shrill hell and Barim barred all Belcontis from the labs. She counter-attacked, rapier against bludgeon, and got her staff back in the labs. They were to observe only, for science and the record.

Jealous, scared, we'll show 'em up, the Mordin lab men laughed. And so we will, by the bones of Great Russel!

Craig saw Miss Ames several times around the labs. She was a tall, slender woman and she looked pinch-mouthed and unhappy. She detached Sidis from ringwalling and made him a lab observer. Craig thought a lot about what Midori had told him. He especially liked that notion of resorption and waited for his chance to spring it at the mess table. It came one morning at breakfast. Wilde's crew shared a table with lab men in the raftered, stone-floored mess hall. It was always a clamour of voices and rattling mess gear. Craig sat between Cobb and Jordan and across from a squat, bald-headed lab man named Joe Breen. Joe brought up the subject of ringwalls and Craig saw his chance.

'Them ringwalls, how they make 'em,' he said. 'They eat themselves and grow themselves again; it's called resorption.'

'They're resorbing sons of guns, for sure,' Joe said. 'How do you like the way they mate?'

'That way's not for me!' Wilde shouted from the head of the table.

'What do they mean?' Craig whispered it to Jordan, but Cobb heard him.

'Blanky wants to know the facts of life,' Cobb said loudly. 'Who'll tell him?'

'Who but old Papa Bork?' Wilde shouted. 'Blanky, when a flitterbug gets that funny feeling it rounds up from one to a dozen others. They clump on a stem and get resorbed into one of those pinkish swellings you're all the time seeing. After a while it splits and a mess of crawlers falls out. Get it?'

37

Craig blushed and shook his head.

'They crawl off and plant themselves and each one grows into a phytogenous stem,' Jordan said. 'For a year it buds off new phytos like mad. Then it turns into a vegetative stem.'

'Hell, I seen plenty crawlers,' Craig muttered. 'I just didn't know they was seeds.'

Cobb snickered. 'Know how to tell the boy crawlers from the girl crawlers, Blanky?' he asked. Joe Breen laughed.

'You're sharp as a gunflint, ain't you, Cobb?' Jordan said. 'You don't tell their sex, Craig, you count it. They got one pair of legs for each parent.'

'Hey, you know, that's good!' Wilde said. 'Maybe a dozen sexes, each one tearing a slow piece off all the others in one operation. That's good, all right!'

'Once in a lifetime, it better be good,' Joe said. 'But Great Russel, talk about polyploidy and multihybrids — wish we could breed *Thanasis* that way.'

'I'll breed my own way,' Wilde said. 'Just you give me the chance.'

'These Belconti women think Mordinmen are crude,' Joe said. 'You'll just have to save it up for Mordin.'

'There's a pretty little target lives alone on Burton Island,' Wilde said.

'Yeah! Blanky knows her,' Cobb said. 'Can she be had, Blanky?'

'No!' Craig clamped his big hand around his coffee cup. 'She's funny, keeps to herself a lot,' he said. 'But she's decent and good.'

'Maybe Blanky never tried,' Cobb said. He winked at Joe. 'Sometimes all you have to do is ask them quiet ones.'

Everyone laughed. Craig scowled and clamped his teeth.

'I'm the guy that'll ask, give me the chance,' Wilde shouted.

'Old Bork'll come at her with them two red dots shining and she'll fall back into loading position slick as gun oil,' Joe said.

'Yeah, and he'll find out old One-dot Cobb done nipped in there ahead of him,' Cobb whooped.

The work horn blared. The men stood up in a clatter of scraping feet and chairs.

'Blanky, you go on brewhouse duty till Monday,' Wilde said. 'Then we start a new field job.'

Craig wished they were back in the field already. He felt a sudden dislike of Base Camp.

*

The new job was dusting translocator pollen over the many North Continent areas where, seen from the air, silver streaking into dark green signalled phyto infiltration of old-strain *Thanasis*. The flowerless killers were wind-pollinated, with the sexes on separate plants. Old ringwall scars made an overlapping pattern across half the continent, more often than not covered by silvery, iridescent strands of pure phyto growth where *Thanasis* had once ravaged. Wilde charted new ringwalls to be blown the next trip out. It was hot, sweaty work in the black protective suits and helmets. They stayed contaminated and ate canned rations and forgot about camp fires. After two weeks their pollen cargo was used up and they landed at Burton Island and spent half a day decontaminating. As soon as he could, Craig broke away and hurried down the gorge path.

He found Midori by the pool. She had been bathing and her yellow print dress moulded damply to her rounded figure and her hair still dripped. Craig couldn't help thinking, what if he'd come a few minutes earlier, and he remembered Cobb's raucous voice saying, sometimes all you have to do is ask them quiet ones. Small phytos, patterned curiously in gold and scarlet and green, clung to Midori's bare arms and shoulders. They looked natural and beautiful, and the gorge and Midori were beautiful, and Craig felt a slow ache inside him.

She was glad to see him. She shook her head sadly when he told her about the translocator pollen. A phyto settled on Craig's hand and he tried to change the subject.

'What makes 'em do that?' he asked. 'The guys think they suck blood, but I know different.'

'They do take body fluid samples, but so tiny you can't feel it.'

'Do they so?' He shook the phyto off his hand. 'Do they really?'

'Tiny, tiny samples,' she said. 'They're curious about us.'

'Just tasting of us, huh?' he shook his head. 'If they can eat us, how come us and pigs and dinotheres can't eat them?'

'Foolish Roy! They don't *eat* us!' She stamped a bare foot. 'They want to understand us, but the only symbols they have are atoms and groups and radicals and ions and so on.' She laughed. 'Sometimes I wonder what they do think of us. Maybe they think we're giant seeds. Maybe they think we're each a single, terribly complicated molecule.' She brushed her lips against a small scarlet and silver phyto on her wrist and it shifted to her cheek. 'This is just their way of trying to live with us,' she said.

'Just the same, it's what we call eating,' he said.

'They eat only water and sunshine. They can't conceive of life that preys on life.' She stamped her foot again. 'Eating! Oh, Roy! It's more like a kiss!'

Craig wished he were a phyto, to touch her smooth arms and shoulders and her firm cheek. He inhaled deeply.

'I know a better kind of kiss,' he said.

'Do you, Roy?' She dropped her eyes.

'Yes, I do,' he said unsteadily. Needles prickled his sweating hands that felt as big as baskets. 'Midori, I — someday I — '

'Yes, Roy?' Her voice was soft.

'Ho the camp!' roared a voice from up the path.

It was Wilde, striding along, grinning with his horse teeth.

'Pop Toyama's throwing us a party, come along,' he shouted. He looked closely at Midori and whistled. 'Hey there, pretty little Midori, you look good enough to eat,' he said.

'Thank you, Mr Wilde.' The small voice was cold.

On the way up the path, Wilde told Midori, 'I learned the *Tanko* dance on Belconti. I told Pop if he'd play, you and I'd dance it for him after we eat.'

'I don't feel at all like dancing,' Midori said.

Wilde and Cobb flanked Midori at the dinner table and vied in paying rough court to her afterwards in the small sitting room. Craig talked to Helen Toyama in a corner. She was a plump, placid woman and she pretended not to hear the rough hunting stories Jordan, Rice and Whelan were telling each other. Papa Toyama kept on his feet, pouring the hot wine. He looked thin and old and fragile. Craig kept watching Midori. Wilde was getting red-faced and loud, and he wouldn't keep his hands off Midori. He gulped bowl after bowl of wine. Suddenly he stood up, left hand still on Midori's shoulder.

'Hey, a toast!' he shouted. He raised his bowl. 'On your feet, men! Guns up for pretty little Midori!'

They stood and drank. Wilde broke his bowl with his hands. He put one fragment in his pocket and handed another to Midori. She shook her head, refusing it. Wilde grinned.

'We'll see a lot of you folks soon,' he said. 'Meant to tell you, Barim's moving you in to Base Camp. Our lab men will fly over next week to pick out what they can use of your gear.'

Papa Toyama's lined, gentle face paled.

'We have always understood that Burton Island would remain a sanctuary for the study of the phytozoa,' he said.

'It was never a Mordin understanding, Pop.'

Toyama looked helplessly from Midori to Helen.

'How much time have we to close our projects?' he asked.

Wilde shrugged. 'Say a month, if you need that long.'

'We do, and more.' Anger touched the old man's voice. 'Why can't we at least stay here until the Belconti relief ship comes?'

'This has been our home for twenty years,' Helen said softly.

'I'll ask the Huntsman to give you all the time he can,' Wilde said, more gently. 'But as soon as he pulls a harvest of pure-line translocator seed out of the forcing chambers, he wants to seed this island. We figure to get a maximum effect in virgin territory.'

Papa Toyama blinked and nodded.

'More wine?' he asked, looking around the room.

When Wilde and Midori danced, Papa Toyama's music sounded strange to Craig. It sounded as sad as the piping of phytos.

*

These translocator hybrids were sure deathific, the lab men chortled. Their free-systems had high thermal stability; that would get around that sneaky phyto trick of running a fever. Their recombination index was fantastic. But there'd be a time lag in gross effect, of course. The phytos were still infiltrating more and more old-strain *Thanasis* areas. Belconti bastards should've started translocation years ago, the lab men grumbled.

41

Scared, making their jobs last, want this planet for themselves. But wait. Just wait.

Craig and Jordan became good friends. One afternoon Craig sat waiting for Jordan at a table in the cavernous, smoky beer hall. On the rifle range an hour earlier he had fired three perfect Great Russel patterns and beaten Jordan by ten points. Barim had chanced by, slapped Craig's shoulder, and called him 'stout rifle'. Craig glowed at the memory. He saw Jordan coming with the payoff beer, threading between crowded, noisy tables and the fire pit where the pig carcass turned. Round face beaming, Jordan set four bottles on the rough plank table.

'Drink up, hunter!' he said. 'Boy, today you earned it!'

Craig grinned back at him and took a long drink.

'My brain was ice,' he said. 'It wasn't like me doing it.'

Jordan drank and wiped his mouth on the back of his hand.

'That's how it takes you when it's for real,' he said. 'You turn into one big rifle.'

'What's it like, Jordan? What's it really like, then?'

'Nobody can ever say.' Jordan looked upward into the smoke. 'You don't eat for two days, they take you through the hunt ceremonies, you get to feeling light-headed and funny, like you don't have a name or a family any more. Then —' His nostrils flared and he clenched his fists. 'Then — well, for me — there was Great Russel coming at me, getting bigger and bigger, filling the whole world, just him and me in the world.' Jordan's face paled and he closed his eyes. 'That's the moment. Oh, oh, oh — that's the moment!' he said. He sighed, then looked at Craig solemnly. 'I fired the pattern like it was somebody else, the way you just said. Three-sided and I *felt* it hit wide, but I picked it up with a spare.'

Craig's heart thudded. He leaned forward.

'Were you scared then, even a least little bit?'

'You ain't scared then, because you're Great Russel himself.' Jordan leaned forward too, whispering. 'You feel your own shots hit you, Craig, and you know you can't never be scared again. It's like a holy dance you and Great Russel been practicing for a million years. After that, somewhere inside you, you never stop doing that dance until you die.'

Jordan sighed again, leaned back and reached for his bottle.

'I dream about it lots,' Craig said. He noticed his hands were shaking. 'I wake up scared and sweating. Well, anyway, I mailed my application to the Hunt College by the ship you came here on.'

'You'll gun through, Craig. Did you hear the Huntsman call you "stout rifle"?'

'Yeah, like from a long way off.' Craig grinned happily.

'Move your fat rump, Jordan!' a jovial voice shouted.

It was Joe Breen, the bald, squat lab man. He had six bottles clasped in his hairy arms. Sidis came behind him. Joe put down his bottles.

'This is Sidis, my Belconti seeing eye,' he said.

'We know Sidis; he's an old ringwaller,' Jordan said. 'Hi, Sidis.'

'Hello, Jordan, Roy,' Sidis said. 'Don't see you around much.'

He and Joe sat down. Joe uncapped bottles.

'We're in the field most all the time now,' Craig said.

'You'll be out more, soon's we pull the pure-line translocator seed,' Joe said. 'It's close. Sidis has kittens every day.'

'You grow 'em, we'll plant 'em,' Jordan said. 'Sidis, why don't you get off Joe's neck and come ringwalling again?'

'Too much to learn here in the labs,' Sidis said. 'We're all going to make our reputations out of this, if Joe and his pals don't kill us before we can publish.'

'Damn the labs. Give me the field,' Jordan said. 'Right, Craig?'

'Right. It's clean and good, out with the phytos,' Craig said. 'This resorption they got, does away with things being rotten and dead—'

'Well, arrow my guts!' Joe slammed down his bottle. 'Beer must make you poetical, Blanky,' he snorted. 'What you really mean is, they eat their own dead and their own dung. Now make a poem out of that!'

Craig felt the familiar weak, helpless anger rise in him.

'With them everything is alive all the time without stopping,' he said. 'All you can say they eat is water and sunshine.'

'They eat water and fart helium,' Joe said. 'Some old-time Belconti, name of Toyama, thought they could catalyse hydrogen fusion.'

'They do,' Sidis said. 'They can grow at night and underground and in the winter. When you stop to think about it, they're pretty wonderful.'

'You're a damned poet too,' Joe said. 'All you Belcontis are poets.'

'We're not, but I wish we had more poets,' Sidis said. 'Roy, you haven't forgotten what I told you once?'

'I ain't a poet,' Craig said. 'I never rhymed two words in my life.'

'Craig's all right. Barim called him "stout rifle" on the range this afternoon,' Jordan said. 'Joe, that guy Toyama, he's still here, out on Burton Island. We got orders to move him in to Base Camp on our next field trip.'

'Great Russel, he must've been here twenty years!' Joe said. 'How's he ever stood it?'

'Got his wife along,' Jordan said. 'Craig here is going on three years. He's standing it.'

'He's turning into a damned poet,' Joe said. 'Blanky, you better go home for sure on the next relief ship, while you're still a kind of a man.'

*

Craig found Midori alone in her house. It looked bare. Her paintings lay strapped together besides crates of books and clothing. She smiled at him, but she looked tired and sad.

'It's hard, Roy. I don't want to leave here,' she said. 'I can't bear to think of what you're going to do to this island.'

'I never think about what we do, except that it just has to be,' he said. 'Can I help you pack?'

'I'm finished. We've worked for days. And now Barim won't give us transportation for our cases of specimens.' She was almost ready to cry. 'Papa Toyama's heart is broken,' she said.

Craig bit his lip. 'Heck, we can carry fifty tons,' he said. 'We got the room. Why don't I ask Mr Wilde to take 'em anyway?'

She grasped his arms and looked up at him.

'Would you, Roy? I—don't want to ask him a favour. The cases are stacked outside the lab building.'

Craig found his chance after supper at the Toyamas'. Wilde left off paying court to Midori and carried his wine bowl outside. Craig followed and asked him. Wilde was looking up at the sky. Both moons rode high in a clear field of stars.

'What's in the cases, did you say?' Wilde asked.

'Specimens, slides, and stuff. It's kind of like art to 'em.'

'All ours now. I'm supposed to destroy it,' Wilde said. 'Oh hell! All right, if you want to strong-back the stuff aboard.' He chuckled. 'I about got Midori talked into taking one last walk down to that pool of hers. I'll tell her you're loading the cases.' He nudged Craig. 'Might help, hey?'

When he had the forty cases stowed and lashed, Craig lifted the flyer to a hundred feet to test his trim. Through his side window he saw Wilde and Midori come out of the Toyama house and disappear together down the gorge path. Wilde had his arm across her shoulders. Craig grounded and went back, but he couldn't rejoin the party. For an hour he paced outside in dull, aching anger. Then his crewmates came out, arguing noisily.

'Ho Craig! Where been, boy?' Jordan slapped his shoulder. 'I just bet Cobb you could outgun him tomorrow, like you did me. We'll stick him for the beer.'

'Like hell,' Cobb said.

'Like shooting birds in a cage,' Jordan said. 'Come along, Craig. Get some sleep.'

'I ain't sleepy,' Craig said.

'Bet old Bork's shooting a cage bird about now,' Cobb said. They all laughed except Craig.

'Come along, Craig,' Jordan said. 'You got to be slept and rested for tomorrow. If you don't outgun Cobb, I'll disown you.'

'All right, but I ain't sleepy,' Craig said.

On the trip to Base Camp next morning Craig stayed at the controls and had no chance to speak to Midori. He wasn't sure he wanted a chance. Cobb outgunned him badly on the range and he drank himself sodden afterwards. He woke next morning to Jordan's insistent shaking.

'We're going out again right away,' Jordan said. 'Don't let Bork catch you sleeping in. Something went wrong for him last night over in Belconti quarters and he's mad as a split snake.'

Four hours later Craig grounded the flyer again at the Burton Island station, with a cargo of pure-line translocator seed. The crew wore black pro-suits. Craig felt dizzy and sick. Wilde seemed very angry. He ordered his men to seed all the paths and open spaces around the buildings. Craig and Jordan seeded the gorge path and the area around the pool. When they finished, they rested briefly on the quartz boulder. For the first time, Craig let himself look around. Phytos danced piping above their heads. The stems marching up the slopes transmuted the golden sun glare to a strong, silvery moonlight that sparkled on the quartz ledge and the cascading water. He wondered if he'd ever see it again. Not like this, anyway.

'Say, it's pretty down here,' Jordan said. 'Kind of twangs your string, don't it? It'll make a nice hunting camp someday.'

'Let's go up,' Craig said. 'They'll be waiting.'

When he lifted out of the field, Craig looked down at the station from his side window. Midori's house looked small and forlorn and accusing.

*

Months of driving fieldwork followed. At Base Camp six men died of a mutant free-system before an immunizer could be synthesized. An escaped control virus wiped out a seed crop. The once jovial atmosphere turned glum and the Mordin lab men muttered about Belconti sabotage. On his first free day Craig checked out a sports flyer, found Midori in the Belconti quarters, and asked her to go riding. She came, wearing a white blouse and pearls and a blue-and-yellow flared skirt. She seemed sad, her small face half dreaming and her eyes unfocused. Craig forgot about being angry with her and wanted to cheer her. When he was a mile up and heading south, he tried.

'You look pretty in that dress, like a phyto,' he said.

She smiled faintly. 'My poor phytos. How I miss them,' she said. 'Where are we going, Roy?'

'Russel Island, down ahead there. I want you to see Great Russel.'

'I want to see him,' she said. A moment later she cried out and grasped his arm. 'Look at that colour in the sky over to the right!'

It was a patch of softly twinkling, shifting colours far off and high in the otherwise cloudless sky.

'Migratory phytos,' he said. 'We see 'em all the time.'

'I know,' she said. 'Let's go up close. Please, Roy.'

He arrowed the flyer towards the green-golden cloud. It resolved into millions of phytos, each with its opalescent hydrogen sac inflated and drifting northwest in the trade wind.

'They stain the air with beauty,' Midori said. She was almost crying, but her face was vividly awake and her eyes sparkled. 'Go clear inside, please, Roy.'

She used to look like that when she was painting in the gorge, Craig thought. It was the way he liked her best. He matched wind speed inside the cloud and lost all sense of motion. Vividly coloured phytos obscured land, sea and sky. Craig felt dizzily suspended in nowhere and moved closer to Midori. She slid open her window to let in the piping and the spicy perfume.

'It's so beautiful I can't bear it,' she said. 'They have no eyes, Roy. We must know for them how beautiful they are.'

She began piping and trilling in her clear voice. A phyto patterned in scarlet and green and silver dropped to her outstretched hand and she sang to it. It deflated its balloon and quivered velvety wings. Craig shifted uneasily.

'It acts almost like it knows you,' he said.

'It knows I love it.'

He frowned. 'Love, something so different, that ain't how I mean love.'

She looked up. 'How do you understand love, Roy?'

'Well, you want to protect people you love, do things for 'em,' he said. He was blushing. 'What can you do for a phyto?'

'Stop trying to exterminate them,' she said softly.

'Please don't start that again,' he said. 'I don't like to think about it either, but I know it just has to be.'

'It will never be,' she said. 'I know. Look at all the different colour patterns out there. Papa Toyama remembers when phytos were almost all green. They developed the new pigment patterns to make counter-substances against *Thanasis*.' She lowered her voice. 'All the colours and patterns are new thoughts in that strange, inconceivably powerful biochemical mind of theirs. This cloud is a message, from one part of it to another part of it. Doesn't it frighten you?'

'You do, I think.' He moved slightly away from her. 'I didn't know they been changing like that.'

'Who stays here long enough to notice? Who looks around him to see?' Her lips trembled. 'But just think of the agony and the changings, through all the long years men have been trying to kill this planet. What if something – somehow – suddenly *understands*?'

Craig felt the hair bristle on his neck and he shifted further away from her. He felt weird and alone, without time or place or motion in that piping, perfumed phyto cloud-world. He couldn't face Midori's eyes.

'Damn it, this planet belongs to Great Russel!' he said harshly. 'We'll win yet. At least they'll never take back Base or Russel Islands. Their seeds can't walk on water.'

She kept her eyes on his, judging or pleading or questioning, he couldn't tell. He couldn't bear them. He dropped his own eyes.

'Shake that thing off your hand!' he ordered. 'Close your window. I'm getting out of here!'

*

Half an hour later Craig hovered the flyer over the wholesome green grass and honest oak trees of Russel Island. He found Great Russel and held him in the magniviewer and they watched him catch and kill a buffalo. Midori gasped.

'Ten feet high at the shoulder. Four tons, and light on his feet as a cat,' Craig said proudly. 'That long reddish hair is like wire. Them bluish bare spots are like armour plate.'

'Aren't his great teeth enough to kill the cattle he eats?' she asked. 'What enemies has he, to need those terrible horns and claws?'

'His own kind. And us,' Craig said. 'Our boys will hunt him here, here on this planet, and become men. Our men will hunt him here, to heal their souls.'

'You love him, don't you, Roy? Did you know you were a poet?' She couldn't take her eyes off the screen. 'He *is* beautiful, fierce and terrible, not what women call beauty.'

'He's a planet-shaker, he is! It takes four perfect shots to bring him down,' Craig said. 'He jumps and roars like the world ending – oh, Midori, I'll have my day!'

'But you might be killed.'

'The finest kind of death. In our lost-colony days, our old

fathers fought with bow and arrow,' Craig said. 'Even now, sometimes, we form a sworn band and fight him to the death with spears and arrows.'

'I've read of sworn bands. I suppose you can't help how you feel.'

'I don't want to help it. A sworn band is the greatest honour that can come to a man,' he said. 'But thanks for trying to understand.'

'I want to understand,' she said. 'I want to, Roy. Is it that you can't believe in your own courage until you face Great Russel?'

'That's just what women can't ever understand.' He looked at her eyes again and that question or whatever was still in them. 'Girls can't help turning into women, but a man has to make himself,' he said. 'It's like I don't have my man's courage until I get it from Great Russel. There's chants and stuff with salt and fire — afterwards the boy eats pieces of the heart — I shouldn't talk about that, you'll laugh.'

'I feel more like crying,' she said. 'There are different kinds of courage, Roy.' Her face worked strangely, but she kept her eyes on his. 'You have more courage than you know, Roy. You must find your true courage in your own heart, not in Great Russel's.'

'I can't.' He clenched his fists and looked away from her eyes. 'I'm just a nothing inside me, until I face Great Russel,' he said.

'Take me home, Roy, I'm afraid I'm going to cry.' She dropped her face to her folded hands. 'I don't have much courage,' she said.

They flew to Base Camp in silence. When Craig helped her down from the flyer, she was really crying. She bowed her head momentarily against his chest and the spicy phyto smell rose from her hair.

'Goodbye, Roy,' she said.

He could barely hear her. Then she turned and ran.

*

Craig didn't see her again. Wilde's crew spent all its time in the field, blowing ringwalls and planting translocator seed. Craig was glad to be away. The atmosphere of Base Camp turned from glum to morose. Everywhere across North Continent new phyto growth in silver, green and scarlet spotted the dark green *Thanasis* areas. Other ringwall crews reported the same of Main and South continents. Wilde's temper became savage; Cobb cursed bitterly at trifles; even happy-go-lucky Jordan stopped joking. Half asleep one night in a field camp, Craig heard Wilde shouting incredulous questions at the communicator inside the flyer. He came out cursing to rouse the camp.

'Phytos are on Base Island,' he said. 'Stems popping up everywhere.'

'Great Russel in the sky!' Jordan jerked full awake. 'How come?'

'Belconti bastards planted 'em, that's how!' Wilde said. 'Barim's got 'em all arrested under camp law.'

Cobb began cursing in a steady, monotonous voice.

'That — cracks — the gunflint!' Jordan said.

'We can't turn loose *Thanasis* there,' Whelean said. 'What'll we do?'

'Kill 'em by hand,' Wilde said grimly. 'We'll sow the rest of our seed broadcast and go in to help.'

Craig felt numb and unbelieving. Shortly after noon he grounded the flyer at Base Camp, in the foul area beyond the emergency rocket-launching frame. Wilde cleaned up at once and went to see Barim, while his crew decontaminated the flyer. When they came through the irradiation tunnel in clean denims, Wilde was waiting.

'Blanky, come with me!' he barked.

Craig followed him into the grey stone building at the field edge, Wilde pushed him roughly through a door, said 'Here he is, Huntsman,' and closed the door again.

Rifles, bows and spears decorated the stone walls. The burly Chief Huntsman, cold-eyed under his roached grey hair and the four red dots, sat facing the door from behind a wooden desk. He motioned Craig to sit down in one of the row of wooden chairs along the inner wall. Craig sat stiffly in the one nearest the door. His mouth was dry.

'Roy Craig, you are on your trial for life and honour under camp law,' Barim said sternly. 'Swear now to speak truth in the blood of Great Russel.'

'I swear to speak truth in the blood of Great Russel.' Craig's voice sounded squeaky and false to him. He began to sweat.

'What would you say of someone who deliberately betrayed our project to destroy the phytos?'

'He would be guilty of hunt treason, sir, and be outlawed.'

'Very well.' Barim clasped his hands and leaned forward, his grey eyes boring into Craig's eyes. 'What did you tell Bork Wilde was in those cases you flew from Burton Island to Base Island?'

Craig felt his stomach knot up.

'Slides, specimens, science stuff, sir,' he said.

Barim questioned him closely about the cases. Craig tried desperately to speak the truth without naming Midori. Barim forced her name from him, then questioned him on her attitudes. Craig sweated and squirmed and a terrible fear grew in him. He kept his eyes on Barim's eyes and spoke a tortured kind of truth, but he would not attaint Midori. Finally Barim broke their locked gazes and slapped his desk.

'Are you in *love* with Midori Blake, boy?' he roared.

Craig dropped his own glance. 'I don't know,' he said. How do you know when you're in love, he thought. You just know it, like you know you're alive. 'Well—I like to be around her—I guess I never thought—' he said. If you have to think about it, it ain't love, it's just being friends, he thought. 'I—don't think so, sir,' he said finally.

'The phyto seeds came here in those cases,' Barim said. 'Who planted them?'

Craig avoided Barim's eyes. 'They can walk and plant themselves, sir. Maybe they escaped,' he said. His mouth was dry as powder.

'Would Midori Blake be morally capable of releasing them?'

Craig's face twisted. 'Morally—I'm not clear on the word, sir—' Sweat dripped on his hands.

'I mean, would she have the guts to want to do it and to do it?'

Ice clamped Craig's heart. He looked Barim in the eye.

'No, sir!' he said. 'I won't never believe that about Midori!'

Barim smiled grimly and slapped his desk again.

'Wilde!' he roared. 'Bring them in!'

Midori, in white blouse and black skirt, came in first. Her face was pale but composed, and she smiled faintly at Craig.

Mildred Ames followed, slender and thin-faced in white, then Wilde, scowling blackly. Wilde sat between Craig and Miss Ames, Midori on the end.

'Miss Blake, young Craig has clearly been your dupe, as you insist he has,' Barim said. 'Your confession ends your trial except for sentencing. Once more I beg you to say why you have done this.'

'You wouldn't understand,' Midori said. 'Be content with what you know.'

Her voice was low but firm. Craig felt sick with dismay.

'I can't understand without condoning,' Barim said. 'For your own sake, I must know your motive. You may be insane.'

'You know I'm sane,' Midori said. 'You know that.'

'Yes.' Barim's wide shoulders sagged. 'Invent a motive, then,' he said. He seemed almost to plead. 'Say you hate Mordin. Say you hate me.'

'I hate no one. I'm sorry for you all.'

'I'll give you a reason!' Miss Ames jumped to her feet, thin face burning. 'Your reckless, irresponsible use of translocation endangers us all! Accept defeat and go home!'

She helped Barim recover his composure. He smiled.

'Please sit down, Miss Ames,' he said calmly. 'In three months your relief ship will take you to safety. But we neither accept defeat nor fear death. We will require no tears of you or anyone.'

Miss Ames sat down, her whole posture shouting defiance. Barim swung his eyes back to Midori and his face turned to iron.

'Miss Blake, you are guilty of hunt treason. You have betrayed your own kind in a fight with an alien life form,' he said. 'Unless you admit to some recognizably *human* motive, I must conclude that you abjure your own humanity.'

Midori said nothing. Craig stole a glance at her. She sat erect but undefiant, small feet together, small hands folded in her lap. Barim slapped his desk and stood up.

'Very well. Under camp law I sentence you, Midori Blake, to outlawry from your kind. You are a woman and not of Mordin; therefore I will remit the full severity. You will be set down, lacking everything made with hands, on Russel Island. There you may still be nourished by the roots and berries of the Earth-type life you have wilfully betrayed. If you survive until the Belconti relief ship comes, you will be sent home on it.' He burned his glance at Midori. 'Have you anything to say before I cause your sentence to be executed?'

The four red dots blazed against the sudden pallor of the Huntsman's forehead. Something snapped in Craig. He leaped up, shouting into the hush.

'You can't do it, sir! She's little and weak! She doesn't know our ways –'

'Down! Shut up, you whimpering fool!' Wilde slapped and wrestled Craig down to his chair. 'Silence!' Barim thundered. Wilde sat down, breathing hard, and the room was hushed again.

'I understand your ways too well,' Midori said. 'Spare me your mercy. Put me down on Burton Island.'

'Midori, no!' Miss Ames turned to her. 'You'll starve! *Thanasis* will kill you!'

'You can't understand either, Mildred,' Midori said. 'Mr Barim, will you grant my request?'

Barim leaned forward, resting on his hands. 'It is so ordered,' he said huskily. 'Midori Blake, almost you make me know again the taste of fear.' He straightened and turned to Wilde, his voice suddenly flat and impersonal. 'Carry out the sentence, Wilde.'

Wilde stood up and pulled Craig to his feet. 'Get the crew to the flyer. Wear pro-suits,' he ordered. '*Run*, boy!'

Craig stumbled out into the twilight.

Craig drove the flyer northwest from Base Camp at full throttle, overtaking the sun, making it day again. Silence ached in the main cabin behind him. He leaned away from it, as if to push the flyer forward with his muscles. He refused to think at all, but he couldn't help feeling. He knew it had to be and still he couldn't bear it. It seemed an anguished forever before he grounded the flyer roughly beside the deserted buildings on Burton Island. They got out, the men in black pro-suits, Midori still in blouse and skirt. They stood apart quietly and looked towards her little house on the cliff edge. *Thanasis* thrust up dark green and knee high along all the paths.

'Break out ringwall kits. Blow all the buildings,' Wilde ordered. 'Blanky, you come with me.'

At Midori's house Wilde ordered Craig to sink explosive

pellets every three feet along the foundations. A single pellet would have been enough. Craig found his voice.

'The Huntsman didn't say to do this, Mr Wilde. Can't we at least leave her this house?'

'She won't need it,' Wilde said. '*Thanasis* will kill her before morning.'

'Let her have it to die in, then. She loved this little house.'

Wilde grinned without mirth, baring his big horse teeth.

'She's *outlaw*, Blanky,' he said. 'You know the law: nothing made with hands.'

Craig bowed his head, teeth clamped. Wilde whistled tunelessly as Craig set the pellets. They returned to the flyers and Jordan reported the other buildings ready to blow. His round, jolly face was grim. Midori had not moved. Craig wanted to speak to her, say he was sorry, say goodbye, but he knew if he tried he would find no words but a howl. Her strange little smile seemed already to remove her to another world, a million light-years from Roy Craig and his kind. Cobb looked at her, his rat face eager.

'We'll detonate from the air,' Wilde said. 'The blast will kill anyone standing here.'

'We're supposed to take off all her clothes first,' Cobb said. 'You know the law, Bork. Nothing made with hands.'

'That's right,' Wilde said.

Midori took off her blouse. She looked straight at Wilde. Red mist clouded Craig's vision.

'Load the kits,' Wilde said abruptly. 'Into the flyer, all hands! *Jump*, you dogs!'

From his side window by the controls Craig saw Midori start down the gorge path. She walked as carelessly relaxed as if she were going down to paint. *Thanasis* brushed her bare legs and he thought he saw the angry red spring out. She did not flinch or look back. Craig felt the pain in his own skin. He lifted the flyer with a lurching roar and he did not look out when Wilde blew up the buildings.

Away from the sun, southeast towards Base Camp, wrapped in his own thought-vacant hell, Roy Craig raced to meet the night.

*

With flame, chemicals and grub hoes, the Mordinmen fought their losing battle for Base Island. Craig worked himself groggy with fatigue to keep from thinking. He felt a mingled sense of loss and grief and anger and satisfaction, and he wondered if he were losing his mind. The phyto stems radiated underground with incredible growth energy. They thrust up redoubly each new day like hydra heads. Newly budded phytos, the size of thumbnails, coloured the air of Base Island in gaily dancing swirls. Once Craig saw Joe Breen, the squat lab man, cursing and hopping like a frog while he slashed at dancing phytos with an axe. It seemed to express the situation.

Barim made his grim decision to move camp to Russel Island and seed the home island with *Thanasis*. Craig was helping erect the new camp when he collapsed. He awoke in bed in a small, bare infirmary room at Base Camp. The Mordin doctor took blood samples and questioned him. Craig admitted to nausea and joint pains for several days past.

'I been half crazy, sir,' he defended himself. 'I didn't know I was sick.'

'I've got twenty more do know it,' the doctor grunted.

He went out, frowning. Craig slept, to flee in dream-terror from a woman's eyes. He half woke at intervals for medication and clinical tests, to sleep again and face repeatedly a Great Russel dinothere. It looked at him with a woman's inscrutable eyes. He roused into the morning of the second day to find another bed squeezed into the small room, by the window. Papa Toyama was in it. He smiled at Craig.

'Good morning, Roy,' he said. 'I would be happier to meet you in another place.'

Many were down and at least ten had died, he told Craig. The Belconti staff was back in the labs, working frantically to identify agent and vector. Craig felt hollow and his head ached and he didn't much care. Dimly he saw Miss Ames in a white lab smock come around the foot of his bed to stand between him and Papa Toyama. She took the old man's hand.

'George, old friend, we've found it,' she said.

'You do not smile, Mildred.'

'I don't smile. All night I've been running a phase analysis of diffraction patterns,' she said. 'It's what we've feared—a spread of two full Ris units.'

'So. Planet Froy again.' Papa Toyama's voice was calm. 'I would like to be with Helen now, for the little time we have.'

'Surely,' she said. 'I'll see to it.'

Quick, heavy footsteps sounded outside. A voice broke in.

'Ah. Here you are, Miss Ames.'

Barim, in leather hunting clothes, bulked in the door. Miss Ames turned to face him across Craig's bed.

'I'm told you found the virus,' Barim said.

'Yes.' Miss Ames smiled thinly.

'Well, what countermeasures? Twelve are dead. What can I do?'

'You might shoot at it with a rifle, Mr Barim. It is a *Thanasis* free-system that has gotten two degrees of temporal freedom. Does that mean anything to you?'

His heavy jaw set like a trap. 'No, but your manner does. It's the plague, isn't it?'

She nodded. 'No suit can screen it. No cure is possible. We are all infected.'

Barim chewed his lip and looked at her in silence.

'For your sake now, I wish we'd never come here,' he said at last. 'I'll put our emergency rocket in orbit to broadcast a warning message. That will save your relief ship, when it comes, and Belconti can warn the sector.' A half smile softened his bluff, grim features. 'Why don't you rub my nose in it? Say you told me so?'

'Need I?' Her chin up. 'I pity you Mordinmen. You must all die now without dignity, crying out for water and your mothers. How you will loathe that!'

'Does that console you?' Barim still smiled. 'Not so, Miss Ames. All night I thought it might come to this, and even now men are forging arrow points. We'll form a sworn band and all die fighting Great Russel.' His voice deepened and his eyes blazed. 'We'll stagger who can, crawl who must, carry our helpless, and all die fighting like men.'

'Like savages! No! No!' Her hands flew up in shocked protest. 'Forgive me for taunting you, Mr Barim. One never says

Yes to death. I need your help, all of your men and transport, truly I do. Some of us may live, if we fight hard enough.'

'How?' He growled it. 'I thought on Planet Froy—'

'Our people on Planet Froy had only human resources,' she said. 'But here, I'm certain that somewhere already the phytos have synthesized the plague immunizer that seems forever impossible to human science.' Her voice shook. 'Please help us, Mr Barim. If we can find it, isolate enough to learn its structure—'

'No!' He cut her off bluntly. 'Too long a gamble. One doesn't run squealing away from death, Miss Ames. My way's decent and sure.'

Her chin came up again and her voice sharpened. 'How dare you condemn your own men unconsulted? They might prefer a fight for life.'

'Hah! You don't know them!' He bent to shake Craig's shoulder with rough affection. 'You, lad,' he said. 'You'll get up and walk with a sworn band, won't you?'

'No,' Craig said.

He struggled off his pillow, propped shakily on his arms. Miss Ames smiled and patted his cheek.

'You'll stay and help us fight to live, won't you?' she said.

'No,' Craig said.

'Think what you say, lad!' Barim said tautly. 'Great Russel can die of plague, too. We owe him a clean death.'

Craig sat bolt upright. He stared straight ahead.

'I foul the blood of Great Russel,' he said slowly and clearly. 'I foul it with dung. I foul it with carrion. I foul it with—'

Barim's fist knocked Craig to the pillow and split his lip. The Huntsman's face paled under his tan.

'You're mad, boy!' he whispered. 'Not even in madness may you say those words.'

Craig struggled up again. 'You're the crazy ones, not me,' he said. He tongued his lip and blood dripped on his thin pyjama coat. 'I'll die an outlaw, that's how I'll die,' he said. 'An outlaw, on Burton Island.' He met Barim's unbelieving eyes. 'I foul the blood—'

'Silence!' Barim roared. 'Outlawry it is. I'll send a party for you, stranger.'

He whirled and stamped out. Miss Ames followed him.

'You Mordinmen,' she said, shaking her head.

Craig sat on the edge of his bed and pulled his sweat-soaked pyjamas straight. The room blurred and swam around him. Papa Toyama's smile was like a light.

'I'm ashamed. I'm ashamed. Please forgive us, Papa Toyama,' Craig said. 'All we know is to kill and kill and kill.'

'We all do what we must,' the old man said. 'Death cancels all debts, Roy. It will be good to rest.'

'Not my debts. I'll never rest again,' Craig said. 'All of a sudden I know — Great Russel, *how* I know — I know I loved Midori Blake.'

'She was a strange girl,' Papa Toyama said. 'Helen and I thought she loved you, in the old days on our island.' He bowed his head. 'But our lives are only chips in a waterfall. Goodbye, Roy.'

Jordan in a black pro-suit came shortly after. His face was bitter with contempt. He jerked his thumb at the door.

'On your feet, stranger! Get going!' he snapped.

In pyjamas and barefooted, Craig followed him. From somewhere in the infirmary he heard a voice screaming. It sounded like Cobb. They walked across the landing field. Everything seemed underwater. Men were rigging to fuel the emergency rocket. Craig sat apart from the others in the flyer. Cobb was missing. Wilde was flushed and shivering and his eyes glared with fever. Jordan took the controls. No one spoke. Craig dozed through coloured dream-scraps while the flyer outran the sun. He woke when it grounded in early dawn at Burton Island.

He climbed down and stood swaying beside the flyer. *Thanasis* straggled across the rubble heaps and bulked waist-high in the dim light along the paths. Phytos stirred on their stems and piped sleepily in the damp air. Craig's eyes searched for something, a memory, a presence, a completion and rest, he didn't know, searching with his eyes, but he felt it very near him. Then Wilde came behind him, shoving. Craig moved away.

'Stranger!' Wilde called.

Craig turned and looked into the fever-glaring eyes above the big horse teeth. The teeth gaped.

'I foul the blood of Midori Blake. I foul it with dung. I—'

Strength from nowhere exploded into the bone and muscle of Roy Craig. He sprang and felt the teeth break under his knuckles. Wilde fell. The others scrambled down from the flyer.

'Blood right! Blood right!' Craig shouted.

A bell note rang in this voice, as strange to him as the strength that flamed along his nerves. Jordan held back Rice and Whelan. Wilde rose, spitting blood, swinging big fists. Craig closed to meet him, berserk in fury. The world wheeled and tilted, shot with flashing colours, gasping with grunts and curses, but rock-steady in the centre of things, Wilde pressed the fight and Craig hurled it back on him. He felt the blows without pain, felt his ribs splinter, felt the good shock of his own blows all the way to his heels. Bruising falls on the rough slag, feet stamping, arms grappling, hands tearing, breath sobbing, both men on knees clubbing with fists and forearms. The scene cleared and Craig saw through one eye Wilde crumpled and inert before him. He rose unsteadily. He felt weightless and clean inside.

'Blood right, stranger,' Jordan said, grim faced and waiting.

'Let it go,' Craig said. 'Great Russel go with you, stranger.'

He turned down the gorge path, ignoring his chest pains, crashing through the rank *Thanasis. Home!* going *home!* going *home!* a bell tolled in his head. He did not look back.

Thanasis grew more sparsely in the shaded gorge. Craig heard the waterfall and old memories cascaded upon him. He rounded to view of it by the quartz boulder and his knees buckled and he knelt beside the boulder. She was very near him. He felt an overpowering sense of her presence. She was this place.

Dawn light shafted strongly into the gorge, sparkled on the quartz ledge, made fleeting rainbows in the spray above the pool. Phytos lifted from ghost-silver stems to twitter and dance their own rainbow in the air. Something rose in Craig's throat and choked him. Tears blurred his good eye.

'Midori,' he said. 'Midori.'

The feeling overwhelmed him. His heart was bursting. He could find no words. He raised his arms and battered face to the sky and cried out incoherently. Then a blackness swept away his intolerable pain.

Titanic stirrings. Windy rushings. Sharp violences swarming.

Fittings-together in darkness. A trillion times a trillion a trillion patient searchings. Filtering broken lights, silver, green, golden, scarlet.

Bluntings. Smoothings. Transformings into otherness.

Flickering awareness, planet-vast and atom-tiny, no focus between. The proto-sensorium of a god yearning to know himself. Endless, patient agony in search for being.

Form and colour outfolding in middle focus. Flashings of terrible joy and love unspeakable. It looked. Listened. Felt. Smelled. Tasted.

Crystalline polar wastes. Wine of sweet. Warm sun glint on blue water. Perfumed wind caress. Thorn of bitter. Rain patter. Silver-green sweep of hill. Storm roar and shaking. Sharp of salt. Sleeping mountains. Surf beat. Star patterns dusted on blackness. Clear of sour. Cool moons of night.

It knew and loved.

Ragged line of men gaunt under beard stubble. Green plain. High golden sun. Roar. Shaggy redness bounding. Bow twangs. Whispering arrow flights. Deep-chested shouts of men. Lances thrusting. Bodies ripped, thrown, horn-impaled and beating with fists. Great shape kneeling, threshing, streaming blood. Deep man-shouts dwindling to a silence.

It knew and sorrowed.

The woman bathing. Sunlight dappling rounded limbs. Black hair streaming. Grace beyond bearing. Beauty that was pain.

It shook terribly with love.

Ground firm beneath rested flesh, whole and unblemished forever. Bursting excitement. HOME! coming HOME! coming HOME!

It came home.

Roy Craig knew his body again and the solid frame of things around him. He lay on his back and a warm, aromatic breeze blew down the gorge and tossed the branches in graceful, silvery patterns against the blue sky. He heard the waterfall and the phytos and he felt rested and good. He groped for an old, lost grief and it was lost forever in Midori suddenly kneeling beside him, her face radiant and her fingers cool on his forehead. Except for clinging phytos, she was naked. He was naked too and he was not ashamed and not excited and he realized they were both dead. He sat up in fearful wonder.

'Midori,' he said. 'When you die – it's like this – how – what –'

He wanted to know a million things, but one came first.

'Can I ever lose you again, now?' he asked.

'Never again.' She smiled. 'We didn't die, Roy. We're more alive than we've ever been.'

He took her hands. They were warm and solid.

'The plague killed everybody,' he said.

'I know. You talked in your delirium. But we didn't die.'

'What happened to us?'

'The phytos saved us,' she said. 'Somewhere in their infinite life-spectrum they matched up a band for humans. They mingled their substance with ours, cleansed us of *Thanasis* and gave us immunity.' She smiled and squeezed his hands. 'I know how you feel. I watched over you for two weeks while phytos came and went from you. Then I understood what had happened to me.'

His hand discovered his beard and he nodded. 'I have to believe you. But why, when we tried so long and hard to kill 'em? Why?'

'They couldn't know that. Here death and decay are only vital changings,' she said. 'This life never split apart, Roy, and in wholeness is nothing but love.'

'I felt – dreamed that.' He told her of his visions.

'It was no dream,' she said. 'You were diffused into the planetary consciousness. It happened to me, too.'

'I'm afraid I'm dreaming right this minute,' he said. 'Can we still eat and drink and all?'

She laughed, jumped to her feet and pulled him upright.

'Foolish Roy. You still don't believe you're alive,' she said. 'Come, I want to show you something.'

He ran hand in hand with her to the pool side. The gravel hurt his feet, but the scrubby *Thanasis* that brushed his ankles didn't hurt at all. Beside the pool, stems had fused ringwall fashion into a series of connecting rooms like hollow cones, clean, dry and silvery with shadows. He followed Midori through the rooms and outside again to where a grove of separate stems displayed brownish swellings. She tore away one covering like thin paper to reveal pearly, plum-sized nodules closely packed in a cavity. She held one to his lips and he ate it. It was cool and crisp, with a delightful, unfamiliar flavour. He realized he was very hungry. He ate another and looked at her with awe.

'There are hundreds of these vesicles,' she said. 'No two ever taste quite the same.'

'Do they know us like people, then?' he asked. 'Like I know you?'

'It knows us biochemically, as if we were giant molecules,' she said. 'Here's what I think, Roy. I think this life had infinite potentialities and mastered its environment using only the tiniest part of them. It never split up, to fight itself and evolve that way. So it lay dreaming and might have dreamed forever —'

She looked away across the pool to the stem clad slope and the dancing, rainbow clouds of phytos.

'Go on,' he said. 'You mean we came then, with *Thanasis*?'

'Yes. We forced changes, genetic recombinations, rises in temperatures and process speeds. Whatever happened at one point could be duplicated everywhere, because it's all one and a year is to it like a million years in the evolution of Earth-life. It raised itself to a new level of awareness. We awakened it.' She brought her eyes back to Craig's eyes. 'I feel it knows us and loves us for that.'

'Loves us for *Thanasis*!'

'It loves *Thanasis* too. *Thanasis* is being fused into the planetary life, just as we are,' she said. 'It thinks us biochemically, Roy. Like each littlest phyto, we are thoughts now in that strange mind. I think we focus its new-found awareness somehow, serve it as a symbol system, a form-giver —' She lowered her voice and pressed closer to him and he felt her warmth and nearness. 'We are its thoughts that also think themselves, the first it has ever had,' she whispered. 'It is a great and holy mystery, Roy. Only through us can it know its own beauty and wonder. It loves and needs us.'

'I feel what you mean.' He ran his hands down the smooth

curve of her back and she shivered under his hands. 'I feel what you mean. I know what you mean.' He clasped her to him and kissed her. 'I love it, too. Through you, I love it.'

'I give you back its love,' she whispered into his shoulder.

'We're alive!' he said. 'Midori, now I know we're alive!'

'We're alive. Do you realize that we'll never be ill, never grow old, never have to die?'

He pressed his face into her hair. 'Never is a long time. But I want you for a long, long time, Midori.'

'Our children will take up our duties,' she said, still into his shoulder, and she was blushing now. 'If we tire, we can be resorbed and diffuse through the planetary consciousness, as we did in our visions.'

'Our children,' he said. 'Our children's children. Thousands and thousands. It's wonderful, Midori.'

'It could be the same for any old or ill human being who might come to this planet, now,' she said. 'They could have youth and strength again forever.'

'Yes.' He looked up at the arching sky. 'And there's a rocket up there in orbit with a warning message. Maybe they'll discover us someday. But for a long time yet they'll hunt shy of us like the plague they think we are.'

'Yes. It's not fair they can't know —'

'That they are their own plague,' he finished for her.

He kissed her tear-bright eyes and patted her head to rest again on his shoulder.

The secret place

This morning my son asked me what I did in the war. He's fifteen and I don't know why he never asked me before. I don't know why I never anticipated the question.

He was just leaving for camp, and I was able to put him off by saying I did government work. He'll be two weeks at camp. As long as the counsellors keep pressure on him, he'll do well enough at group activities. The moment they relax it, he'll be off studying an ant colony or reading one of his books. He's on astronomy now. The moment he comes home, he'll ask me again just what I did in the war, and I'll have to tell him.

But I don't understand just what I did in the war. Sometimes I think my group fought a death fight with a local myth and only Colonel Lewis realized it. I don't know who won. All I know is that war demands of some men risks more obscure and ignoble than death in battle. I know it did of me.

It began in 1931, when a local boy was found dead in the desert near Barker, Oregon. He had with him a sack of gold ore and one thumb-sized crystal of uranium oxide. The crystal ended as a curiosity in a Salt Lake City assay office until, in 1942, it became of strangely great importance. Army agents traced its probable origin to a hundred-square-mile area near Barker. Dr Lewis was called to duty as a reserve colonel and ordered to find the vein. But the whole area was overlain by thousands of feet of Miocene lava flows and of course it was geological insanity to look there for a pegmatite vein. The area had no drainage pattern and had never been glaciated. Dr Lewis protested that the crystal could have gotten there only by prior human agency.

It did him no good. He was told his not to reason why. People very high up would not be placated until much money and scientific effort had been spent in a search. The army sent him young geology graduates, including me, and demanded progress reports. For the sake of morale, in a kind of frustrated desperation, Dr Lewis decided to make the project a model textbook exercise in mapping the number and thickness of the basalt beds over the search area all the way down to the prevolcanic Miocene surface. That would at least be a useful addition to Columbia Plateau lithology. It would also be proof positive that no uranium ore existed there, so it was not really cheating.

That Oregon countryside was a dreary place. The search area was flat, featureless country with black lava outcropping everywhere through scanty grey soil in which sagebrush grew hardly knee high. It was hot and dry in summer and dismal with thin snow in winter. Winds howled across it at all seasons. Barker was about a hundred wooden houses on dusty streets, and some hay farms along a canal. All the young people were away at war or war jobs, and the old people seemed to resent us. There were twenty of us, apart from the contract drill crews who lived in their own trailer camps, and we were gown against town, in a way. We slept and ate at Colthorpe House, a block down the street from our headquarters. We had our own 'gown' table there, and we might as well have been men from Mars.

I enjoyed it, just the same. Dr Lewis treated us like students, with lectures and quizzes and assigned reading. He was a fine teacher and a brilliant scientist, and we loved him. He gave us all a turn at each phase of the work. I started on surface mapping and then worked with the drill crews, who were taking cores through the basalt and into the granite thousands of feet beneath. Then I worked on taking gravimetric and seismic readings. We had fine team spirit and we all knew we were getting priceless training in field geophysics. I decided privately that after the war I would take my doctorate in geophysics. Under Dr Lewis, of course.

In early summer of 1944 the field phase ended. The contract drillers left. We packed tons of well logs and many boxes of gravimetric data sheets and seismic tapes for a move to Dr Lewis's Midwestern university. There we would get more months of valuable training while we worked our data into a set of structure contour maps. We were all excited and talked a lot about being with girls again and going to parties. Then the army said part of the staff had to continue the field search. For technical compliance, Dr Lewis decided to leave one man, and he chose me.

It hit me hard. It was like being flunked out unfairly. I thought he was heartlessly brusque about it.

'Take a jeep run through the area with a Geiger once a day,' he said. 'Then sit in the office and answer the phone.'

'What if the army calls when I'm away?' I asked sullenly.

'Hire a secretary,' he said. 'You've an allowance for that.'

So off they went and left me, with the title of field chief and only myself to boss. I felt betrayed to the hostile town. I decided I hated Colonel Lewis and wished I could get revenge. A few days later old Dave Gentry told me how.

He was a lean, leathery old man with a white moustache and I sat next to him in my new place at the 'town' table. Those were grim meals. I heard remarks about healthy young men skulking out of uniform and wasting tax money. One night I slammed my fork into my half-emptied plate and stood up.

'The army sent me here and the army keeps me here,' I told the dozen old men and women at the table. 'I'd like to go overseas and cut Japanese throats for you kind hearts and gentle people, I really would! Why don't you all write your Congressman?'

I stamped outside and stood at one end of the verandah, boiling. Old Dave followed me out.

'Hold your horses, son,' he said. 'They hate the government, not you. But government's like the weather, and you're a man they can get aholt of.'

'With their teeth,' I said bitterly.

'They got reasons,' Dave said. 'Lost mines ain't supposed to be found the way you people are going at it. Besides that, the Crazy Kid mine belongs to us here in Barker.'

He was past seventy and he looked after horses in the local feedyard. He wore a shabby, open vest over faded suspenders and grey flannel shirts and nobody would ever have looked for wisdom in that old man. But it was there.

'This is big, new, lonesome country and it's hard on people,' he said. 'Every town's got a story about a lost mine or a lost gold cache. Only kids go looking for it. It's enough for most folks just to know it's there. It helps 'em stand the country.'

'I see,' I said. Something stirred in the back of my mind.

'Barker never got its lost mine until thirteen years ago,' Dave said. 'Folks just naturally can't stand to see you people find it this way, by main force and so soon after.'

'We know there isn't any mine,' I said. 'We're just proving it isn't there.'

'If you could prove that, it'd be worse yet,' he said. 'Only you can't. We all saw and handled that ore. It was quartz, just rotten with gold in wires and flakes. The boy went on foot from his house to get it. The lode's got to be right close by out there.'

He waved toward our search area. The air above it was luminous with twilight and I felt a curious surge of interest. Colonel Lewis had always discouraged us from speculating on that story. If one of us brought it up, I was usually the one who led the hooting and we all suggested he go over the search area with a dowsing rod. It was an article of faith with us that the vein did not exist. But now I was all alone and my own field boss.

We each put up one foot on the verandah rail and rested our arms on our knees. Dave bit off a chew of tobacco and told me about Owen Price.

'He was always a crazy kid and I guess he read every book in town,' Dave said. 'He had a curious heart, that boy.'

I'm no folklorist, but even I could see how myth elements were already creeping into the story. For one thing, Dave insisted the boy's shirt was torn off and he had lacerations on his back.

'Like a cougar clawed him,' Dave said. 'Only they ain't never been cougars in that desert. We backtracked that boy till his trail crossed itself so many times it was no use, but we never found one cougar track.'

I could discount that stuff, of course, but still the story gripped me. Maybe it was Dave's slow, sure voice; perhaps the queer twilight; possibly my own wounded pride. I thought of how great lava upwellings sometimes tear loose and carry along huge masses of the country rock. Maybe such an erratic mass lay out there, perhaps only a few hundred feet across and so missed by our drill cores, but rotten with uranium. If I could find it, I would make a fool of Colonel Lewis. I would discredit the whole science of geology. I, Duard Campbell, the despised and rejected one, could do that. The front of my mind shouted that it was nonsense, but something far back in my mind began composing a devastating letter to Colonel Lewis and comfort flowed into me.

'There's some say the boy's youngest sister could tell where he found it, if she wanted,' Dave said. 'She used to go into that desert with him a lot. She took on pretty wild when it happened and then was struck dumb, but I hear she talks again now.' He shook his head. 'Poor little Helen. She promised to be a pretty girl.'

'Where does she live?' I asked.

'With her mother in Salem,' Dave said. 'She went to business school and I hear she works for a lawyer there.'

*

Mrs Price was a flinty old woman who seemed to control her daughter absolutely. She agreed Helen would be my secretary as soon as I told her the salary. I got Helen's security clearance with one phone call; she had already been investigated as part of tracing that uranium crystal. Mrs Price arranged for Helen to stay with a family she knew in Barker, to protect her reputation. It was in no danger. I meant to make love to her, if I had to, to charm her out of her secret, if she had one, but I would not harm her. I know perfectly well that I was only playing the game called 'The Revenge of Duard Campbell'. I knew I would not find any uranium.

Helen was a plain little girl and she was made of frightened ice. She wore low-heeled shoes and cotton stockings and plain dresses with white cuffs and collars. Her one good feature was her flawless fair skin against which her peaked, black Welsh eyebrows and smoky blue eyes gave her an elfin look at times. She liked to sit neatly tucked into herself, feet together, elbows in, eyes cast down, voice hardly audible, as smoothly self-contained as an egg. The desk I gave her faced mine and she sat like that across from me and did the busy work I gave her, and I could not get through to her at all.

I tried joking and I tried polite little gifts and attentions, and I tried being sad and needing sympathy. She listened and worked and stayed as far away as the moon. It was only after two weeks and by pure accident that I found the key to her.

I was trying the sympathy gambit. I said it was not so bad, being exiled from friends and family, but what I could not stand was the dreary sameness of that search area. Every spot was like every other spot and there was no single, recognizable *place* in the whole expanse. It sparked something in her and she roused up at me.

'It's full of just wonderful places,' she said.

'Come out with me in the jeep and show me one,' I challenged.

She was reluctant, but I hustled her along regardless. I guided the jeep between outcrops, jouncing and lurching. I had our map photographed on my mind and I knew where we were every minute, but only by map coordinates. The desert had our marks on it: well sites, seismic blast holes, wooden stakes, cans, bottles and papers blowing in that everlasting wind, and it was all dismally the same anyway.

'Tell me when we pass a "place" and I'll stop,' I said.

'It's all places,' she said. 'Right here's a place.'

I stopped the jeep and looked at her in surprise. Her voice was strong and throaty. She opened her eyes wide and smiled; I had never seen her look like that.

'What's special, that makes it a place?' I asked.

She did not answer. She got out and walked a few steps. Her whole posture was changed. She almost danced along. I followed and touched her shoulder.

'Tell me what's special,' I said.

She faced around and stared right past me. She had a new grace and vitality and she was a very pretty girl.

'It's where all the dogs are,' she said.

'Dogs?'

I looked around at the scrubby sagebrush and thin soil and ugly black rock and back at Helen. Something was wrong.

'Big, stupid dogs that go in herds and eat grass,' she said. She kept turning and gazing. 'Big cats chase the dogs and eat them. The dogs scream and scream. Can't you hear them?'

'That's crazy!' I said. 'What's the matter with you?'

I might as well have slugged her. She crumpled instantly back into herself and I could hardly hear her answer.

'I'm sorry. My brother and I used to play out fairy tales here. All this was a kind of fairyland to us.' Tears formed in her eyes. 'I haven't been here since ... I forgot myself. I'm sorry.'

*

I had to swear I needed to dictate 'field notes' to force Helen into the desert again. She sat stiffly with pad and pencil in the jeep while I put on my act with the Geiger and rattled off jargon. Her lips were pale and compressed and I could see her fighting against the spell the desert had for her, and I could see her slowly losing.

She finally broke down into that strange mood and I took good care not to break it. It was weird but wonderful, and I got a lot of data. I made her go out for 'field notes' every morning and each time it was easier to break her down. Back in the office she always froze again and I marvelled at how two such different persons could inhabit the same body. I called her two phases 'Office Helen' and 'Desert Helen'.

I often talked with old Dave on the verandah after dinner. One night he cautioned me.

'Folks here think Helen ain't been right in the head since her brother died,' he said. 'They're worrying about you and her.'

'I feel like a big brother to her,' I said. 'I'd never hurt her, Dave. If we find the lode, I'll stake the best claim for her.'

He shook his head. I wished I could explain to him how it was only a harmless game I was playing and no one would ever find gold out there. Yet, as a game, it fascinated me.

Desert Helen charmed me when, helplessly, she had to uncover her secret life. She was a little girl in a woman's body. Her voice became strong and breathless with excitement and she touched me with the same wonder that turned her own face vivid and elfin. She ran laughing through the black rocks and scrubby sagebrush and momentarily she made them beautiful. She would pull me along by the hand and sometimes we ran as much as a mile away from the jeep. She treated me as if I were a blind or foolish child.

'No, no, Duard, that's a cliff!' she would say, pulling me back.

She would go first, so I could find the stepping stones across streams. I played up. She pointed out woods and streams and cliffs and castles. There were shaggy horses with claws, golden birds, camels, witches, elephants and many other creatures. I pretended to see them all, and it made her trust me. She talked and acted out the fairy tales she had once played with Owen. Sometimes he was enchanted and sometimes she, and the one had to dare the evil magic of a witch or giant to rescue the other. Sometimes I was Duard and other times I almost thought I was Owen.

Helen and I crept into sleeping castles, and we hid with pounding hearts while the giant grumbled in search of us and we fled, hand in hand, before his wrath.

Well, I had her now. I played Helen's game, but I never lost sight of my own. Every night I sketched in on my map whatever I had learned that day of the fairyland topography. Its geomorphology was remarkably consistent.

When we played, I often hinted about the giant's treasure. Helen never denied it. She would put her finger to her lips and look at me with solemn, round eyes.

'You only take the things nobody cares about,' she would say. 'If you take the gold or jewels, it brings you terrible bad luck.'

'I got a charm against bad luck and I'll let you have it too,' I said once. 'It's the biggest, strongest charm in the whole world.'

'No. It all turns into trash. It turns into goat beans and dead snakes and things,' she said crossly. 'Owen told me. It's a rule, in fairyland.'

Another time we talked about it as we sat in a gloomy ravine near a waterfall. We had to keep our voices low or we would wake up the giant. The waterfall was really the giant snoring and it was also the wind that blew forever across that desert.

'Doesn't Owen ever take anything?' I asked.

I had learned by then that I must always speak of Owen in the present tense.

'Sometimes he has to,' she said. 'Once right here the witch had me enchanted into an ugly toad. Owen put a flower on my head and that made me be Helen again.'

'A really truly flower? That you could take home with you?'

'A red-and-yellow flower bigger than my two hands,' she said. 'I tried to take it home, but all the petals came off.'

'Does Owen ever take anything home?'

'Rocks, sometimes,' she said. 'We keep them in a secret nest in the shed. We think they might be magic eggs.'

I stood up. 'Come and show me.'

She shook her head vigorously and drew back. 'I don't want to go home,' she said. 'Not ever.'

She squirmed and pouted, but I pulled her to her feet.

'Please, Helen, for me,' I said. 'Just for one little minute.'

I pulled her back to the jeep and we drove to the old Price place. I had never seen her look at it when we passed it and she did not look now. She was freezing fast back into Office Helen. But she led me around the sagging old house with its broken windows and into a tumbledown shed. She scratched away some straw in one corner, and there were the rocks. I did not realize how excited I was until disappointment hit me like a blow in the stomach.

They were worthless waterworn pebbles of quartz and rosy granite. The only thing special about them was that they could never have originated on that basalt desert.

*

After a few weeks we dropped the pretence of field notes and simply went into the desert to play. I had Helen's fairyland almost completely mapped. It seemed to be a recent fault block mountain with a river parallel to its base and a gently sloping plain across the river. The scarp face was wooded and cut by deep ravines and it had castles perched on its truncated spurs. I kept checking Helen on it and never found her inconsistent. Several times when she was in doubt I was able to tell her where she was, and that let me even more deeply into her secret life. One morning I discovered just how deeply.

She was sitting on a log in the forest and plaiting a little basket out of fern fronds. I stood beside her. She looked up at me and smiled.

'What shall we play today, Owen?' she asked.

I had not expected that, and I was proud of how quickly I

rose to it. I capered and bounded away and then back to her and crouched at her feet.

'Little sister, little sister, I'm enchanted,' I said. 'Only you in all the world can uncharm me.'

'I'll uncharm you,' she said, in that little girl voice. 'What are you, brother?'

'A big, black dog,' I said. 'A wicked giant named Lewis Rawbones keeps me chained up behind his castle while he takes all the other dogs out hunting.'

She smoothed her grey skirt over her knees. Her mouth drooped.

'You're lonesome and you howl all day and you howl all night,' she said. 'Poor doggie.'

I threw my head back and howled.

'He's a terrible, wicked giant and he's got all kinds of terrible magic,' I said. 'You mustn't be afraid, little sister. As soon as you uncharm me I'll be a handsome prince and I'll cut off his head.'

'I'm not afraid.' Her eyes sparkled. 'I'm not afraid of fire or snakes or pins or needles or anything.'

'I'll take you away to my kingdom and we'll live happily ever afterwards. You'll be the most beautiful queen in the world and everybody will love you.'

I wagged my tail and laid my head on her knees. She stroked my silky head and pulled my long black ears.

'Everybody will love me.' She was very serious now. 'Will magic water uncharm you, poor old doggie?'

'You have to touch my forehead with a piece of the giant's treasure,' I said. 'That's the only onliest way to uncharm me.'

I felt her shrink away from me. She stood up, her face suddenly crumpled with grief and anger.

'You're not Owen, you're just a man! Owen's enchanted and I'm enchanted too and nobody will ever uncharm us!'

She ran away from me and she was already Office Helen by the time she reached the jeep.

*

After that day she refused flatly to go into the desert with me. It looked as if my game was played out. But I gambled that Desert Helen could still hear me, underneath somewhere, and

I tried a new strategy. The office was an upstairs room over the old dance hall and, I suppose, in frontier days skirmishing had gone on there between men and women. I doubt anything went on as strange as my new game with Helen.

I always had paced and talked while Helen worked. Now I began mixing common-sense talk with fairyland talk and I kept coming back to the wicked giant, Lewis Rawbones. Office Helen tried not to pay attention, but now and then I caught Desert Helen peeping at me out of her eyes. I spoke of my blighted career as a geologist and how it would be restored to me if I found the lode. I mused on how I would live and work in exotic places and how I would need a wife to keep house for me and help with my paper work. It disturbed Office Helen. She made typing mistakes and dropped things. I kept it up for days, trying for just the right mixture of fact and fantasy, and it was hard on Office Helen.

One night old Dave warned me again.

'Helen's looking peaked, and there's talk around. Miz Fowler says Helen don't sleep and she cries at night and she won't tell Miz Fowler what's wrong. You don't happen to know what's bothering her, do you?'

'I only talk business stuff to her,' I said. 'Maybe she's homesick. I'll ask her if she wants a vacation.' I did not like the way Dave looked at me. 'I haven't hurt her. I don't mean any harm, Dave,' I said.

'People get killed for what they do, not for what they mean,' he said. 'Son, there's men in this here town would kill you quick as a coyote, if you hurt Helen Price.'

I worked on Helen all the next day and in the afternoon I hit just the right note and I broke her defences. I was not prepared for the way it worked out. I had just said, 'All life is a kind of playing. If you think about it right, everything we do is a game.' She poised her pencil and looked straight at me, as she had never done in that office, and I felt my heart speed up.

'You taught me how to play, Helen. I was so serious that I didn't know how to play.'

'Owen taught me to play. He had magic. My sisters couldn't play anything but dolls and rich husbands and I hated them.'

Her eyes opened wide and her lips trembled and she was almost Desert Helen right there in the office.

'There's magic and enchantment in regular life, if you look at it right,' I said. 'Don't you think so, Helen?'

'I know it!' she said. She turned pale and dropped her pencil. 'Owen was enchanted into having a wife and three daughters and he was just a boy. But he was the only man we had and all of them but me hated him because we were so poor.' She began to tremble and her voice went flat. 'He couldn't stand it. He took the treasure and it killed him.' Tears ran down her cheeks. 'I tried to think he was only enchanted into play-dead and if I didn't speak or laugh for seven years, I'd uncharm him.'

She dropped her head on her hands. I was alarmed. I came over and put my hand on her shoulder.

'I did speak.' Her shoulders heaved with sobs. 'They made me speak, and now Owen won't ever come back.'

I bent and put my arm across her shoulders.

'Don't cry, Helen. He'll come back,' I said. 'There are other magics to bring him back.'

I hardly knew what I was saying. I was afraid of what I had done, and I wanted to comfort her. She jumped up and threw off my arm.

'I can't stand it! I'm going home!'

She ran out into the hall and down the stairs and from the window I saw her run down the street, still crying. All of a sudden my game seemed cruel and stupid to me and right that moment I stopped it. I tore up my map of fairyland and my letters to Colonel Lewis and I wondered how in the world I could ever have done all that.

After dinner that night old Dave motioned me out to one end of the verandah. His face looked carved out of wood.

'I don't know what happened in your office today, and for your sake I better not find out. But you send Helen back to her mother on the morning stage, you hear me?'

'All right, if she wants to go,' I said. 'I just can't fire her.'

'I'm speaking for the boys. You better put her on that morning stage, or we'll be around to talk to you.'

'All right, I will, Dave.'

I wanted to tell him how the game was stopped now and how I wanted a chance to make things up with Helen, but I thought I had better not. Dave's voice was flat and savage with contempt and, old as he was, he frightened me.

*

Helen did not come to work in the morning. At nine o'clock I went out myself for the mail. I brought a large mailing tube and some letters back to the office. The first letter I opened was from Dr Lewis, and almost like magic it solved all my problems.

On the basis of his preliminary structure contour maps Dr Lewis had gotten permission to close out the field phase. Copies of the maps were in the mailing tube, for my information. I was to hold an inventory and be ready to turn everything over to an army quartermaster team coming in a few days. There was still a great mass of data to be worked up in refining the maps. I was to join the group again and I would have a chance at the lab work after all.

I felt pretty good. I paced and whistled and snapped my fingers. I wished Helen would come, to help on the inventory. Then I opened the tube and looked idly at the maps. There were a lot of them, featureless bed after bed of basalt, like layers of a cake ten miles across. But when I came to the bottom map, of the prevolcanic Miocene landscape, the hair on my neck stood up.

I had made that map myself. It was Helen's fairyland. The topography was point by point the same.

I clenched my fists and stopped breathing. Then it hit me a second time, and the skin crawled up my back.

The game was real. I couldn't end it. All the time the game had been playing me. It was still playing me.

I ran out and down the street and overtook old Dave hurrying towards the feedyard. He had a holstered gun on each hip.

'Dave, I've got to find Helen,' I said.

'Somebody seen her hiking into the desert just at daylight,' he said. 'I'm on my way for a horse.' He did not slow his stride. 'You better get out there in your stink-wagon. If you don't find her before we do, you better just keep on going, son.'

*

I ran back and got the jeep and roared it out across the scrubby sagebrush. I hit rocks and I do not know why I did not break something. I knew where to go and feared what I would find there. I knew I loved Helen Price more than my own life and I knew I had driven her to her death.

I saw her far off, running and dodging. I headed the jeep to intercept her and I shouted, but she neither saw me nor heard me. I stopped and jumped out and ran after her and the world darkened. Helen was all I could see, and I could not catch up with her.

'Wait for me, little sister!' I screamed after her. 'I love you, Helen! Wait for me!'

She stopped and crouched and I almost ran over her. I knelt and put my arms around her and then it was on us.

They say in an earthquake, when the direction of up and down tilts and wobbles, people feel a fear that drives them mad if they can not forget it afterwards. This was worse. Up and down and here and there and now and then all rushed together. The wind roared through the rock beneath us and the air thickened crushingly above our heads. I know we clung to each other, and we were there for each other while nothing else was and that is all I know, until we were in the jeep and I was guiding it back towards town as headlong as I had come.

Then the world had shape again under a bright sun. I saw a knot of horsemen on the horizon. They were heading for where Owen had been found. That boy had run a long way, alone and hurt and burdened.

I got Helen up to the office. She sat at her desk with her head down on her hands and she quivered violently. I kept my arm around her.

'It was only a storm inside our two heads, Helen,' I said, over and over. 'Something black blew away out of us. The game is finished and we're free and I love you.'

Over and over I said that, for my sake as well as hers. I meant and believed it. I said she was my wife and we would marry and go a thousand miles away from that desert to raise our children. She quieted to a trembling, but she would not speak. Then I heard hoofbeats and the creak of leather in the street below and then I heard slow footsteps on the stairs.

Old Dave stood in the doorway. His two guns looked as natural on him as hands and feet. He looked at Helen, bowed over the desk, and then at me, standing beside her.

'Come on down, son. The boys want to talk to you,' he said.

I followed him into the hall and stopped.

'She isn't hurt,' I said. 'The lode is really out there, Dave, but nobody is ever going to find it.'

'Tell that to the boys.'

'We're closing out the project in a few more days,' I said. 'I'm going to marry Helen and take her away with me.'

'Come down or we'll drag you down!' he said harshly. 'We'll send Helen back to her mother.'

I was afraid. I did not know what to do.

'No, you won't send me back to my mother!'

It was Helen beside me in the hall. She was Desert Helen, but grown up and wonderful. She was pale, pretty, aware and sure of herself.

'I'm going with Duard,' she said. 'Nobody in the world is ever going to send me around like a package again.'

Dave rubbed his jaw and squinted his eyes at her.

'I love her, Dave,' I said. 'I'll take care of her all my life.'

I put my left arm around her and she nestled against me. The tautness went out of old Dave and he smiled. He kept his eyes on Helen.

'Little Helen Price,' he said, wonderingly. 'Who ever would've thought it?' He reached out and shook us both gently. 'Bless you youngsters,' he said, and blinked his eyes. 'I'll tell the boys it's all right.'

He turned and went slowly down the stairs. Helen and I looked at each other, and I think she saw a new face too.

That was sixteen years ago. I am a professor myself now, greying a bit at the temples. I am as positivistic a scientist as you will find anywhere in the Mississippi drainage basin. When I tell a seminar student 'That assertion is operationally meaningless', I can make it sound downright obscene. The students blush and hate me, but it is for their own good. Science is the only safe game, and it's safe only if it is kept pure. I work hard at that, I have yet to meet the student I cannot handle.

My son is another matter. We named him Owen Lewis, and

he has Helen's eyes and hair and complexion. He learned to read on the modern sane and sterile children's books. We haven't a fairy tale in the house — but I have a science library. And Owen makes fairy tales out of science. He is taking the measure of space and time now, with Jeans and Eddington. He cannot possibly understand a tenth of what he reads, in the way I understand it. But he understands all of it in some other way privately his own.

Not long ago he said to me, 'You know, Dad, it isn't only space that's expanding. Time's expanding too, and that's what makes us keep getting farther away from when we used to be.'

And I have to tell him just what I did in the war. I know I found manhood and a wife. The how and why of it I think and hope I am incapable of fully understanding. But Owen has, through Helen, that strangely curious heart. I'm afraid. I'm afraid he will understand.

Mine own ways

Walter Cordice was plump and ageing and he liked a quiet life. On what he'd thought was the last day of his last field job before retirement to New Zealand, he looked at his wife in the spy screen and was dismayed.

Life had not been at all quiet while he and Leo Brumm and Jim Andries had been building the hyperspace relay on Planet Robadur — they had their wives along and they'd had to live and work hidden under solid rock high on a high mountain. That was because the Robadurians were asymbolic and vulnerable to culture shock, and the Institute of Man, which had jurisdiction over hominid planets, forbade all contact with the natives. Even after they'd built her the lodge in a nearby peak, Martha was bored. Cordice had been glad when he and Andries had gone into Tau rapport with the communications relay unit.

That had been two months of peaceful isolation during which the unit's Tau circuits copied certain neural patterns in the men to make itself half sentient and capable of electronic telepathy. It was good and quiet. Now they were finished, ready to seal the station and take their pretaped escape capsule back to Earth; only anthropologists from the Institute of Man would ever visit Robadur again.

And Walter Cordice stood in the wrecked lodge and the picture on the illicit spy screen belted him with dismay.

Robadurians were not symbol users. They simply couldn't have raided the lodge. But the screen showed Martha and Willa Brumm and Allie Andries sitting bound to stakes at a forest edge. Martha's blue dress and tight red curls were unruffled. She sat with her stumpy legs extended primly together and her hard, plump pout said she was grimly not believing what she saw either.

Near a stream, across a green meadow starred yellow with flowers, naked and bearded Robadurians dug a pit with sharp sticks. Others piled dry branches. They were tall fellows, lump-muscled under sparse fur, with foreheads and muzzle jaws. One, in a devil mask of twigs and feathers, seemed an overseer. Beside Martha, pert, dark little Allie Andries cried quietly. Willa was straining her white arms against the cords. They knew they were in trouble, all right.

Cordice turned from the screen, avoiding the eyes of Leo Brumm and Jim Andries. In their tan overalls against the silver-and-scarlet décor they seemed as out of place as the dead Robadurian youth at their feet. Leo's chubby, pleasant face looked stricken. Jim Andries scowled. He was a big, loose-jointed man with bold angular features and black hair. They were young and junior and Cordice knew they were mutely demanding his decision.

Decision. He wouldn't retire at stat-8 now, he'd be lucky to keep stat-7. But he'd just come out of rapport and so far he was clear and the law was clear too, very clear: you minimized culture shock at whatever cost to yourself. But abandon *Martha*? He looked down at the Robadurian youth. The smooth ivory skin was free of blue hair except on the crushed skull. He felt his face burn.

'Our wives bathed him and shaved him and made him a pet?' His voice shook slightly. 'Leo...Leo...'

'My fault, sir. I built 'em the spy screen and went to rescue the boy,' Leo said. 'I didn't want to disturb you and Jim in rapport.' He was a chunky, blond young man and he was quite pale now. 'They—well, I take all the blame, sir.'

'The Institute of Man will fix blame,' Cordice said.

My fault, he thought. For bringing Martha against my better judgment. But Leo's violation of the spy-screen ethic did lead directly to illicit contact and — *this mess*! Leo was young, they'd be lenient with him. All right, his fault. Cordice made his voice crisp.

'We minimize,' he said. 'Slag the lodge, get over and seal up the station, capsule home to Earth and report this.'

Jim really scowled. 'I love my wife, Cordice, whatever you think of yours,' he said. 'I'm getting Allie out of there if I have to culture-shock those blue apes to death with a flame jet.'

'You'll do what I say, Andries! You and your wife signed

a pledge and a waiver, remember?' Cordice tried to stare him down. 'The law says she's not worth risking the extinction of a whole species that may someday become human.'

'Damn the law, she's worth it to me!' Jim said. 'Cordice, those blue apes are human now. How else could they raid up here, kill this boy, carry off the women?' He spat. 'We'll drop you to seal the station, keep your hands clean. Leo and I'll get the women.'

Cordice dropped his eyes. Damn his insolence! Still ... Leo could testify Andries forced it ... he'd still be clear ...

'I'll go along, to ensure minimizing,' he said. 'Under protest — Leo, you're witness to that. But slag this lodge right now!'

Minutes later Leo hovered the flyer outside while Cordice played the flame jet on the rock face. Rock steamed, spilled away, fused, and sank into a bubbling, smoking cavity. Under it the dead youth, with his smooth, muscular limbs, was only a smear of carbon. Cordice felt better.

Half an hour later, lower on the same mountain, Leo hovered the flyer above the meadow. The Robadurians all ran wildly into the forest and Jim didn't need to use the flame jet. Leo grounded and the men piled out and Cordice felt his stomach relax. They ran towards the women. Allie Andries was smiling but Martha was shouting something from an angry face. As he stooped to untie Martha the blue horde came back out of the forest. They came yelling and leaping and slashing with wet, leafy branches and the sharp smell ...

Cordice came out of it sick with the awareness that he was tied to a stake like an animal and that it was his life, not his career, he had to save now. He feigned sleep and peered from eyecorners. Martha looked haggard and angry and he dreaded facing her. He couldn't see the others, except Allie Andries and she was smiling faintly — at Jim, no doubt.

Those two kids must escape, Cordice thought.

He must have been unconscious quite a while because sunset flamed in red and gold downvalley and the pit looked finished. It was elliptical, perhaps thirty feet long and three deep. Robadurians were still mounding black earth along the sides and others were piling brush into a circumscribed thicket, roughly triangular. They chattered, but Cordice knew it was only a mood-sharing noise. That was what made it so horrible. They were asymbolic, without speech and prior to good and evil, a natural force like falling water. He couldn't threaten, bribe, or even plead. Despite his snub nose and full lips he could present an impressive face – at home on Earth. But not to such as these.

Beside the pit the devil masker stood like a tall sentry. Abruptly he turned and strode towards Cordice, trailing his wooden spear. Cordice tensed and felt a scream shape itself in him. Then the devil towered lean and muscular above him. He had no little finger on his spear hand. Keen grey eyes peered down through feathers and twigs.

'Cordice, you fool, why did you bring the women?' the devil asked in fluent English. 'Now all your lives are forfeit.'

The scream collapsed in a grateful gasp. With speech Cordice felt armed again, almost free. But Martha spoke first.

'Men need women to inspire them and give them courage!' she said. 'Walto! Tell him who you are! Make him let us go!'

Walto meant she was angry. In affection she called him *Wally Toes*. But as usual she was right. He firmed his jowls and turned a cool stat-7 stare on the devil mask.

'Look here, if you know our speech you must know we never land on a hominid planet,' he said pleasantly. 'There are plenty of other planets. For technical reasons we had to do a job here. It's done. We have stores and tools to leave behind.' He laughed easily. 'Take them and let us go. You'll never see another of us.'

The devil shook his head. 'It's not what we might see, it's what your women have already seen,' he said. 'They know a holy secret and the god Robadur demands your deaths.'

Cordice paled but spoke smoothly. 'I and Andries have been out of touch with the others for two months. I don't know any secret. While we were isolated Brumm built the women a spy screen and rescued that boy –'

'Who was forfeit to Robadur. Robadur eats his children.'

'Arthur was being *tortured* when he broke free and ran,' Martha said. 'I saw *you* there!'

'On your strictly unethical spy screen.'

'Why not? You're only brute animals!'

The devil pressed his spear to her throat. 'Shut up or I'll spear you now!' he said. Martha's eyes blazed defiance.

'No! *Quiet*, Martha!' Cordice choked. His front collapsed. 'Brumm did it all. Kill him and let us *go*!' He twisted in his bonds.

Leo spoke from behind. 'Yes, I did it. Take me and let them go.' His voice was high and shaky too.

'No! Oh please no!' That was Willa, sobbing.

'Stop that!' Jim Andries roared. 'All of us or none! Listen, you behind the feathers, I know your secret. You're a renegade playing god among the asymbolics. But we're here on clearance from the Institute of Man and they'll come looking for us. Your game's up. Let us go and you'll only be charged with causing culture shock.'

The devil grounded his spear and cocked his head. Robadurians around the pit stood up to watch. Martha shrilled into the hush.

'My own brother is with the Institute of Man!'

'I told you shut up!' The devil slapped her with his spear butt. 'I know your brother. Tom Brennan would kill you himself, to keep the secret.'

'*What* secret, Featherface? That you're a god?' Jim asked.

'The secret that man created himself and what man has done, man can undo,' the devil said. 'I'm not Robadur, Andries, but I'm sealed to him from the Institute of Man. The Institute will cover for your deaths. It's done the same on hundreds of other hominid planets, to keep the secret.'

'Roland Krebs! *Rollo*! You struck a lady—'

Like a snake striking, the spear leaped to her throat. She strained her head back and said 'Ah ... ah ... ah ...,' her face suddenly white and her eyes unbelieving.

'Don't hurt her!' Cordice screamed. 'We'll *swear* to forget, if you let us go!'

The devil withdrew his spear and laughed. 'Swear on what, Cordice? Your honour? Your soul?' He spat. 'What man has done, man can undo. You're the living proof!'

'We'll swear by Robadur,' Cordice pleaded.

The devil looked off into the sunset. 'You know, you might.

You just might,' he said thoughtfully. 'We seal a class of boys to Light Robadur tonight; you could go with them.' He turned back. 'You're the leader, Andries. What about it?'

'What's it amount to?' Jim asked.

'It's a ritual that turns animals into humans,' the devil said. 'There are certain ordeals to eliminate the animals. If you're really men you'll be all right.'

'What about the women?' Jim's voice was edgy.

'They have no souls. Robadur will hold you to account for them.'

'You have great faith in Robadur,' Jim said.

'Not faith, Andries, a scientist's knowledge as hard as your own,' the devil said. 'If you put a Robadurian into a barbering machine he wouldn't need faith to get a haircut. Well, a living ritual is a kind of psychic machine. You'll see.'

'All right, we agree,' Jim said. 'But we'll want our wives unhurt. Understand that, Featherface?'

The devil didn't answer. He shouted and natives swarmed around the stakes. Hands untied Cordice and jerked him erect and his heart was pounding so hard he felt dizzy.

'Don't let them hurt you, Wally Toes!'

Fleetingly in Martha's shattered face he saw the ghost of the girl he had married thirty years ago. She had a touch of the living beauty that lighted the face Allie Andries turned on Jim. Cordice said goodbye to the ghost, numb with fear.

*

Cordice slogged up the dark ravine like a wounded bull. He knew the priests chasing him would spear him like the hunted animal he was unless he reached sanctuary by a sacred pool somewhere ahead. Long since Jim and Leo and the terrified Robadurian youths had gone ahead of him. Stones cut his feet and thorns ripped his skin. Leo and Jim were to blame and they were young and they'd live. He was innocent and he was old and he'd die. Not fair. Let them die too. His lungs flamed with agony and at the base of a steep cascade his knees gave way.

Die here. Not fair. He heard the priests coming and his back muscles crawled with terror. Die fighting. He scrabbled in the water for a stone. Face to the spears. He cringed lower.

Jim and Leo came back down the cascade and helped him up it. 'Find your guts, Cordice!' Jim said. They jerked him along, panting and swearing, until the ravine widened to make a still pool under a towering rock crowned red with the last of sunset. Twenty-odd Robadurian youths huddled whimpering on a stony slope at left. Then priests came roaring and after that Cordice took it in flashes.

He had a guardian devil, a monstrous priest with clay in white bars across his chest. White Bar and others drove him up the slope, threw him spread-eagled on his back, and staked down his wrists and ankles with wisps of grass. They placed a pebble on his chest. He tried to remember that these were symbolic restraints and that White Bar would kill him if he broke the grass or dislodged the pebble. Downslope a native boy screamed and broke his bonds and priests smashed his skull. Cordice shuddered and lay very quiet. But when they pushed the thorn through in front of his left Achilles tendon he gasped and drew up his leg. The pebble tumbled off and White Bar's club crashed down beside his head and he died.

He woke aching and cold under starlight and knew he had only fainted. White Bar sat shadowy beside him on an outcrop, club across hairy knees. Downslope the native boys sang a quavering tone song without formed words. They were mood-sharing, expressing sorrow and fearful wonder. I could almost sing with them, Cordice thought. The pebble was on his chest again and he could feel the grass at his wrists and ankles. A stone dug into his back and he shifted position very carefully so as not to disturb the symbols. Nearby but not in view Jim and Leo began to talk in low voices.

Damn them, Cordice thought. They'll live and I'll die. I'm dying now. Why suffer pain and indignity and die anyway? I'll just sit up and let White Bar end it for me. But first —

'Leo,' he said.

'Mr Cordice! Thank heaven! We thought — how do you feel, sir?'

'Bad. Leo — wanted to say — a fine job here. Your name's in for stat-3. Wanted to say — this all my fault. Sorry.'

'No, sir,' Leo said. 'You were in rapport, how could you —'

'Before that. When I let Martha come and so couldn't make

you juniors leave your wives behind.' Cordice paused. 'I owe — Martha made me, in a way, Leo.'

Her pride, he thought. Her finer feelings. Her instant certainty of rightness that bolstered his own moral indecision. So she ruled him.

'I know,' Leo said. 'Willa's proud and ambitious for me, too.'

Martha worked on Willa, Cordice thought. Hinted she could help Leo's career. So she got her spy screen. Well, he *had* been grading Leo much higher than Jim. Martha didn't like Allie's and Jim's attitude

'I'm going to die, boys,' Cordice said. 'Will you forgive me?'

'No,' Jim said. 'You're woman-whipped to a helpless nothing, Cordice. Forgive yourself, if you can.'

'Look here, Andries, I'll remember that,' Cordice said.

'I'm taking Allie to a frontier planet,' Jim said. 'We'll never see a hairless slug like you again.'

Leo murmured a protest. I'll live to get even with Andries, Cordice thought. Damn his insolence! His heel throbbed and the stone still gouged his short ribs. He shifted carefully and it felt better. He hummed the native boys' song deep in his throat and that helped too. He began to doze. If I live I'll grow my body hair again, he thought.

*

Jim's voice woke him: *Cordice! Lie quiet, now!* He opened his eyes to hairy legs all around him and toothed beast faces in torchlight roaring a song and White Bar with club poised trembling-ready and no little finger on his right hand. The song roared over Cordice like thunder, and sparks like tongues of fire rained down to sear his body. He whimpered and twitched but did not dislodge the stone on his chest. The party moved on. Downslope a boy screamed and club thuds silenced him. And again, and Cordice felt sorry for the boys.

'Damn it all, that really hurt!' Jim said.

'This was the ordeal that boy Arthur failed, only he got away,' Leo said. 'Mrs Cordice kept him on the screen until I could rescue him.'

'How'd he act?' Jim asked.

'Trusted me, right off. Willa said he was very affectionate and they taught him all kinds of tricks. But never speech — he got wild when they tried to make him talk, Willa told me.'

I'm affectionate. I know all kinds of tricks, Cordice thought. Downslope the torches went out and the priests were singing with the boys. White Bar, seated again beside Cordice on the outcrop, sang softly too. It was a new song of formed words and it disturbed Cordice. Then he heard footsteps behind his head and Jim spoke harshly.

'Hello, Featherface, we're still around,' Jim said. 'Mrs Cordice called you a name. *Krebs*, wasn't it? Just who in hell are you?'

'Roland Krebs. I'm an anthropologist,' the devil's voice said. 'I almost married Martha once, but she began calling me *Rollo* just in time.'

That guy? Cordice opened his mouth, then closed it. Damn him. He'd pretend a faint, try not to hear.

'You can't share the next phase of the ritual and it's your great loss,' Krebs said. 'Now each boy is learning the name that he will claim for his own in the last phase, if he survives. The men have a crude language and the boys long ago picked up the words like parrots. Now, as they sing with the priests, the words come alive in them.'

'How do you mean?' Jim asked.

'Just that. The words assort together and for the first time *mean*. That's the Robadurian creation myth they're singing.' Krebs lowered his voice. 'They're not here now like you are, Andries. They're present in the immediacy of all their senses at the primal creation of their human world.'

'Our loss? Yes ... our great loss.' Jim sounded bemused.

'Yes. For a long time words have been only a sickness in our kind,' Krebs said. 'But ideas can still assort and mean. Take this thought: we've found hominids on thousands of planets, but none more than barely entered on the symbol-using stage. Palaeontology proves native hominids have been stuck on the threshold of evolving human minds for as long as two hundred million years. But on Earth our own symbol-using minds evolved in about three hundred thousand years.'

'Does mind evolve?' Jim asked softly.

'Brain evolves, like fins change to feet,' Krebs said. 'The hominids can't evolve a central nervous system adequate for symbols. But on Earth, in no time at all, something worked a structural change in one animal's central nervous system greater than the gross, outward change from reptile to mammal.'

'I'm an engineer,' Jim said. 'The zoologists know what worked it.'

'Zoologists always felt natural selection couldn't have worked it so fast,' Kregs said. 'What we've learned on the hominid planets proves it can't. Natural selection might take half a billion years. *Our* fathers took a short cut.'

'All right,' Jim said. 'All right. Our fathers were their own selective factor, in rituals like this one. They were animals and they bred themselves into men. Is that what you want me to say?'

'I want you to feel a little of what the boys feel now,' Krebs said. 'Yes. Our fathers invented ritual as an artificial extension of instinct. They invented a ritual to detect and conserve all mutations in a human direction and eliminate regressions towards the animal norm. They devised ordeals in which normal animal-instinctive behaviour meant death and only those able to sin against instinct could survive to be human and father the next generation.' His voice shook slightly. 'Think on that, Andries! Human and animal brothers born of the same mother and the animals killed at puberty when they failed certain ordeals only human minds could bear.'

'Yes. Our secret. Our *real* secret.' Jim's voice shook too. 'Cain killing Abel through ten thousand generations. That created *me*.'

Cordice shivered and the rock gouged his short ribs.

'Dark Robadur's sin is Light Robadur's grace and the two are one,' Krebs said. 'You know, the Institute has made a science of myth. Dark Robadur is the species personality, instinct personified. Light Robadur is the human potential of these people. He binds Dark Robadur with symbols and coerces him with ritual. He does it in love, to make his people human.'

'In love and fear and pain and death,' Jim said.

'In pain and death. Those who died tonight were animals. Those who die tomorrow will be failed humans who know they die,' Krebs said. 'But hear their song.'

'I hear it. I know how they feel and thank you for that, Krebs,' Jim said. 'And it's only the boys?'

'Yes, the girls will get half their chromosomes from their fathers. They will get all the effect of the selection except that portion on the peculiarly male Y-chromosome,' Krebs said. 'They will remain without guilt, sealed to Dark Robadur. It will make a psychic difference.'

'Ah. And you Institute people *start* these rituals on the hominid planets, make them self-continuing, like kindling a fire already laid,' Jim said slowly. 'Culture shock is a lie.'

'It's no lie, but it does make a useful smokescreen.'

'Ah. Krebs, thank you. Krebs —' Jim lowered his voice and Cordice strained to hear. '— would you say Light Robadur might be a *transhuman* potential?'

'I hope he may go on to become so,' Krebs said. 'Now you know the full measure of our treason. And now I'll leave you.'

His footsteps died away. Leo spoke for the first time.

'Jim, I'm scared. I don't like this. Is this ritual going to make *us* transhuman? What does that mean?'

'We can't know. Would you ask an ape what *human* means?' Jim said. 'Our fathers bred themselves through a difference in kind. Then they stopped, but they didn't have to. I hope one of these hominid planets will breed on through the human to another difference in kind.' He laughed. 'That possibility is the secret we have to keep.'

'I don't like it. I don't want to be transhuman,' Leo said. 'Mr Cordice! Mr Cordice, what do you think?'

Cordice didn't answer. Why let that damned Andries insult him again? Besides, he didn't know what to think.

'He's fainted or dead, poor fat old bastard,' Jim said. 'Leo, all this ritual is doing to you is forcing you to prove your human manhood, just like the boys have to. We have our manhood now only by accident of fertilization.'

'I don't like it,' Leo said. 'That transhuman stuff. It's ... immoral.'

'It's a hundred thousand years away yet,' Jim said. 'But I like it. What I don't like is to think that the history of galactic life is going to head up and halt forever in the likes of old Wally Toes there.'

'He's not so bad,' Leo said. 'I hope he's still alive.'

I am, God damn you both! Cordice thought. They stopped talking.

Downslope the priests' voices faded and the boys sang their worded creation song alone. White Bar went away. The sky paled above the great rock and bright planets climbed to view. Cordice felt feverish. He lapsed into a half-dream.

He saw a fanned network of golden lines. Nodes thickened to become fish, lizards and men. A voice whispered: *All life is a continuum in time. Son to father, the germ worldline runs back unbroken to the primordial ocean. For you life bowed to sex and death. For you it gasped sharp air with feeble lungs. For you it bore the pain of gravity in bones too weak to bear it. Ten thousand of your hairy fathers, each in his turn, won through this test of pain and terror to make you a man.*

Why?

I don't know why.

Are you a man?

What is a man? I'm a man by definition. By natural right. By accident of fertilization. What else is a man?

Two billion years beat against you like surf, Walter Cordice. The twenty thousand fists of your hairy fathers thunder on you as a door. Open the way or be shattered.

I don't know the way. I lost the way.

Through dream mists he fled his hairy fathers. But they in him preserved intact the dry wisps that bound him terribly with the tensile strength of meaning. They steadied the pebble that crushed him under the mountain-weight of symbol. All the time he knew it.

*

By noon of the clouded day thirst was the greater agony. Cordice scarcely heard the popping noises made by the insects that fed on his crusted blood and serum. But he heard every plash and ripple of the priest-guarded water downslope. Heard too, once and again, the death of boys whose animal thirst overpowered their precarious new bondage to the symbol. Only those who can remember that the grass wisps *mean* survive, Cordice thought. Poor damned kids! To be able to suffer and sin against instinct is to live and be human.

Jim's and Leo's voices faded in and out of his fever dreams. His back was numb now, where the rock dug into it.

Rose of sunset crowned the great rock above the pool when White Bar prodded Cordice downslope with his club. Cordice limped and rubbed his back and every joint and muscle of his misused body ached and clamoured for water. Jim and Leo looked well. Cordice scowled silence at their greetings. I'll die without their damned pity, he thought. He moved apart from them into the group of native boys standing by the rock-edged pool. Their thin lips twitched and their flat nostrils flared and snuffled at the water smell. Cordice snuffled too. He saw Krebs, still masked in twigs and feathers, come through the rank of priests and talk to Jim.

'You'll all be thrown into the water, Andries. For the boys, Dark Robadur must swim the body to the bank or they drown. Light Robadur must prevent the body from drinking or they get clubbed. The two must co-act. Understand?'

Jim nodded and Krebs turned back to the priests. These kids can't do it, Cordice thought. I can't myself. He shook the arm of the boy beside him and looked into the frightened brown eyes. *Don't drink*, he tried to say, but his throat was too gummed for speech. He smiled and nodded and pinched his lips together with his fingers. The boy smiled and pinched his own lips. Then all the boys were doing it. Cordice felt a strange feeling wash through him. It was like love. It was as if they were all his children.

Then wetness cooled his body and splashed his face. He dog-paddled and bit his tongue to keep from gulping. White Bar jerked him up the bank again and behind him he heard the terrible cries and the club thuds. Tears stung his eyes.

Then he was limping and stumbling down the dark ravine. At steep places the native youths held his arms and helped him. They came through screening willows and he saw a fire near the brush-walled pit. The three women stood there. They looked all right. Cordice went with the boys towards the pit.

'Wally Toes! Don't let them hurt you!' Martha cried.

'Shut up!' Cordice yelled. The yell tore his gummed throat.

The boys faced outward and danced in a circle around the pit. The priests danced the opposite way in a larger circle and faced inwards. There was ten feet of annular space between the rings. The priests howled and flung their arms. Cordice was very tired. His heel hurt and his back felt humped. Each time they passed, White Bar howled and pointed at him. He saw Martha every time he passed the firelit area. A priest jumped across and pulled the boy next to Cordice into the space between the rings. Cordice had to dance on away, but he heard screams and club thuds. When he came round again he saw them toss a limp body between the dancers into the pit.

They took more boys and made them kneel and did something to them. If the boys couldn't stand it, they killed them. Even if they did stand it, the priests threw them afterwards into the pit. I've got to stand it, Cordice thought. If I don't they'll kill me. Then White Bar howled and leaped and had him.

Threw him to his knees.

Held his right hand on a flat stone.

Pulled aside the little finger.

Bruising it off with a fist axe! Can't STAND it!

Outrage exploded in screaming pain. Hidden strength leaped roaring to almost-action. Then his hairy fathers came and made him be quiet and he stood it. White Bar chewed through the tendons with his teeth and when the finger was off and the stump seared with an ember the priests threw Cordice into the pit.

He felt other bodies thump beside him and his hairy fathers came very near. All around him they grinned and whispered: *You ARE a man. Your way is open.* He felt good, sure and peaceful and strong in a way he had never felt before. He wanted to hold the feeling and he tried not to hear Jim's voice calling him for fear he would lose it. But he had to, so he opened his eyes and got to his feet. Leo and Jim grinned at him.

'I knew you'd make it, old timer, and I'm glad,' Jim said.

Cordice still had the feeling. He grinned and clasped bloody hands with his friends. All around the pit above their heads the piled brush crackled and leaped redly with flame.

Beyond the fire the priests began singing and Cordice could see them dancing in fantastic leaps. The living native boys struggled free of the dead ones and stood up. He counted fourteen. Smoke blew across the pit and the air was thick and suffocating. It was very hot and they all kept coughing and shifting and turning.

Outside the singing stopped and someone shouted a word. One native boy raised his arms and hunted back and forth along the pit edge. He went close and recoiled again.

'They called his name,' Jim said. 'Now he has to go through the fire to claim it. Now he has to break Dark Robadur's most holy *Thou shalt not.*'

Again the shout. Twice the boy stepped up and twice recoiled. His eyes rolled and he looked at Cordice without seeing him. His face was wild with animal fire-fear.

Leo was crying. 'They can't see out there. Let's push him up,' he said.

'No,' Cordice said.

He felt a Presence over the pit. It was anxious and sorrowful. It was familiar and strange and expected and very right. His hairy fathers were no part of it, but they greeted it and spoke through him.

'Robadur, Robadur, give him strength to pass,' Cordice prayed.

A third shout. The boy went up and through the flame in one great leap. Vast, world-lifting joy swirled and thundered through the Presence.

'Jim, do you feel it?' Cordice asked.

'I feel it,' Jim said. He was crying too.

The next boy tried and fell back. He stood rigid in the silence after the third shout. It was a terrible silence. His hair was singed off and his face was blackened and his lips were skinned back over strong white teeth. His eyes stared and they were not human and they were very sad.

'I've *got* to help him,' Leo said.

Jim and Cordice held Leo back. The boy dropped suddenly to all fours. He burrowed under the dead boys who didn't have names either. Vast sorrow infolded and dropped through the Presence. Cordice wept.

Boy after boy went through. Their feet knocked a dark gap in the flaming wall. Then the voice called *Walter Cordice!*

Cordice went up and through the dark gap and the fire was almost gone there and it was easy.

He went directly to Martha. All her bright hardness and pout were gone and she wore the ghost face. It gleamed as softly radiant as the face of little Allie Andries, who still waited for Jim. Cordice drew Martha off into the shadows and they held each other without talking in words. They watched as the others came out and then priests used long poles to push the flaming wall into the pit. They watched the fire die down and they didn't talk and the dancers went away and Cordice felt the Presence go away too, insensibly. But something was left.

'I love you, Martha,' he said.

They both knew he had the power to say that word and the right to have a woman.

Then another long time and when he looked up again the flyer was there. Willa and Allie stood beside it in dim firelight and Krebs was coming towards him.

'Come along, Cordice. I'll dress that hand for you,' Krebs said.

'I'll wait by the fire, Walter,' Martha said.

Cordice followed Krebs into the forest. His nervous strength was leaving him and his legs felt rubbery. He hurt all over and he needed water, but he still felt good. They came to where light gleamed through a hut of interlaced branches. Leo and Jim were already dressed and standing inside by a rough table and chest. Almost at once the plastigel soothed Cordice's cuts and blisters. He dressed and drank sparingly from the cup of water Jim handed him.

'Well, men —' he said. They all laughed.

Krebs was pulling away the twigs and feathers of his mask. Under it he had the same prognathous face as the Robadurian priests. It wasn't ugly at all.

'Cordice, I suppose you know they can regenerate that finger for you back on Earth,' he said. He combed three fingers through his beard, 'Biofield therapists work wonders, these days.'

'I won't bother,' Cordice said. 'When do we swear our oath? I can swear now.'

'No need,' Krebs said. 'You're sealed to Robadur now. You'll keep the secret.'

'I would have anyway,' Jim said.

Krebs nodded. 'Yes. You were always a man.'

They shook hands around and said goodbye. Cordice led the way to the flyer. He walked hard on his left heel to feel the pain and he knew that it is no small thing, to be a man.

Fiddler's Green

On the morning of the fifth day Kinross woke knowing that before the sun went down one of them would be eaten. He wondered what it would be like.

All yesterday the eight dungaree- and khaki-clad seamen had wrangled about it in thirst-cracked voices. Eight chance-spared survivors adrift without food or water in a disabled launch, riding the Indian Ocean swells to a sea anchor. The SS *Ixion*, 6,000-ton tramp sneaking contraband explosives to the Reds in Sumatra, had blown up and sunk in ten minutes the night of 23 December 1959. Fat John Kruger, the radioman, had not gotten off a distress signal. Four days under the vertical sun of Capricorn, off the steamer lanes and a thousand miles from land, no rain and little hope of any, reason enough and time, for dark thinking.

Kinross, lean and wiry in the faded dungarees of an engineer, looked at the others and wondered how it would go. They were in the same general positions as yesterday, still sleeping or pretending to sleep. He looked at the stubbled faces, cracked lips and sunken eyes, and he knew how they felt. Skin tight and wooden, tongue stuck to teeth and palate, the dry throat a horror of whistling breath and every cell in the body clamouring.

Thirst was worse than pain, he thought. Weber's law for pain. Pain increased as the logarithm of what caused it; a man could keep pace. But thirst was exponential. It went up and up and never stopped. Yesterday they had turned the corner and today something had to give.

Little Fay, of the rat face and bulging forehead, had begun it yesterday. Human flesh boiled in sea water, he had said, took up most of the salt and left a nourishing broth fresh enough to drink. Kinross remembered that false bit of sea lore being whispered among the apprentices on his first cruise long years ago, but now it was no tidbit for the morbid curiosity of youth.

It shouldered into the boat like a ninth passenger sitting between him and all the others.

'No leedle sticks, Fay,' the giant Swede Kerbeck had growled. 'If we haf to eat somebody we yoost eat you.'

Kinross looked at Kerbeck now, sitting just to the left on the stern grating with one huge, bronzed arm draped over the useless tiller. He wore a white singlet and khaki pants and Kinross wondered if he was awake. There was no telling about Kruger just across from him either. The radioman had slept that way, with puffy, hairless hands clasped across the ample stomach under the white sweatshirt, for most of the four days. He had not joined in the restless moving about and talking of the others, stirring only to remoisten the handkerchief he kept on top of his almost hairless head.

'You won't eat me!' Fay had squalled. 'Nor draw lots, neither. Let's have a volunteer, somebody that's to blame for this fix.'

Fay had blamed Kerbeck because the boat was not provisioned. The Swede retorted angrily that he knew it had been so when they had left Mossamedes. Fay blamed Kinross because the launch engine was disabled. Kinross, skin crawling, pointed out mildly enough that the battery had been up and the diesel okay two days before the sinking. Then Fay turned on Kruger for failing to send out a distress signal. Kruger had insisted that the blast had cut him off from the radio shack and that if he had not started at once to swing out the launch possibly none of them would have survived.

Kinross looked forward now at Fay sleeping beside the engine. On the opposite side, also asleep, was Bo Bo, the huge Senegalese stoker, clad only in dungaree shorts. It had seemed to Kinross yesterday that Fay had some sort of understanding with the powerful Negro. Bo Bo had rumbled assent to Fay's accusations and so had the three men in the forward compartment.

Kruger, surprisingly, had resolved the threat. Speaking without heat in his high-pitched, penetrating voice, he told them: Touch one of us aft here and all three will fight. Kerbeck had nodded and unshipped the heavy brass tiller.

While they wavered, Kruger went over to the attack. 'Single out one only man, why don't you, Fay? Who's had the most life already? Take the oldest.'

Silva, the wizened, popeyed Portygee in the bow, creaked an outraged protest. Beside him the thick-set Mexican Garcia laughed harshly.

'Okay, then who's going to die soonest? Take the weakest,' said Kruger. 'Take Whelan.'

The kid Whelan, also in the bow, found strength to whimper an agonized plea. Kinross, remembering yesterday, looked at the two men sprawled in the bow. He half thought the Mexican was looking back at him. His stocky, dungaree-clad body seemed braced against the pitch of the boat as it rode the swells, unlike the flaccidity of the old Portygee.

It was Garcia who had said finally, 'You lose, Fay. You'll have to take your chance on drawing lots with the rest of us. I'll line up with Kruger.'

The three men aft had voted against drawing lots but agreed to go along with the majority. Then Kruger found fault with every method suggested, pointing out how fraud could enter. The day wore out in wrangling. Kinross thought back to the curiously unstrained, liquid quality of Kruger's light voice as contrasted with the harsh croaking of the others. He had seemed in better shape than the rest and somehow in control of things.

Just before sunset, when they had put it off until the next day and while Silva was fingering his rosary and praying for rain, the kid Whelan had seen green fields off to port. He shouted his discovery, flailed his body across the gunwale and sank like a stone.

'There you go, Kruger!' Fay had husked bitterly. 'Up to now that fat carcass of yours had one chance in eight.' Kinross remembered his own twinge of regret.

Kinross felt the rising sun sucking at his dry eyeballs and thirst flamed three-dimensionally through him, consuming sense and reason. He knew that today would be the day and that he wanted it so. He glanced forward again and the Mexican was really looking at him out of red-rimmed eyes.

'I know what you're thinking, Kinross,' he called aft. His voice roused the others. They began sitting up.

*

Little Fay led off, head bobbing and jerking, red eyes demanding agreement. 'Draw lots,' he said. 'No more palaver. Right now or none of us will see sunset.'

Kruger agreed. He clinked several shillings in his hand and passed them around to be looked at. Only one was a George V. Blindfold Bo Bo, the stupidest one, he proposed, and let him pick coins out of the bailing bucket one by one. Fay would sit back to back with him and as soon as Bo Bo had a coin up, but before anyone had seen it, Fay would call the name of the man who was to get it. Whoever got the beard would be the victim.

It was agreed. Silva asked for time to pray and Fay mocked at him. The little man perched on the engine housing, his back against Bo Bo, and looked around calculatingly. Kinross could feel the malice in his glance.

'Law of averages,' Kinross was thinking. 'In the middle of the series. Number three or four. Nonsense, of course.'

Apparently Fay thought so too. When the Negro fumbled up the first coin and asked, 'Who get this one?' Fay answered 'I'll take it.' It was a queen, and Kinross hated Fay.

The next one Fay awarded to Bo Bo and the giant black was safe. For the next, while Kinross held his breath, Fay named Kerbeck. Also safe. Each time a sigh went through the boat.

Then the fourth trial and Fay called out 'Kinross'. The engineer blinked his dry eyes and strained to see the coin in the thick black fingers. He knew first from the relief on Silva's face and then he saw it plainly himself. It was the beard.

No one would meet his eyes but Fay and Bo Bo. Kinross hardly knew what he felt. The thought came 'an end of torment' and then 'I'll die clean'. But he still dully resented Fay's nasty air of triumph.

Fay opened his clasp knife and slid the bailing bucket next to the engine. 'Hold him across the engine housing, Bo Bo,' he ordered. 'We can't afford to lose any of the blood.'

'Damn you, Fay, I'm still alive,' Kinross said. His gaunt features worked painfully and his Adam's apple twitched in a futile attempt at swallowing.

'Knock me in the head first, mates,' he pleaded. 'You, Kerbeck, use the tiller.'

'Yah,' said the Swede, still not returning his glance. 'Now yoost wait a leedle, Fay.'

'All of you listen to me,' Kruger said. 'I know a way we can get as much fresh water as we can drink, in just a few minutes, and nobody has to die.' His light voice was effortless, liquid, trickling the words into their startled ears.

*

All hands looked at Kruger, suspicious, half hating him for his cool voice and lack of obvious suffering. Kinross felt a thrill of hope.

'I mean it,' Kruger said earnestly. 'Cold, fresh water is all around us, waiting for us, if we only knew one little thing that we can't quite remember. You felt it all yesterday. You feel it now.'

They stared. Fay ran his thumb back and forth along the edge of the clasp knife. Then Garcia said angrily, 'You're nuts, Kruger. Your gyro's tumbled.'

'No, Garcia,' Kruger said, 'I was never saner. I knew this all the time, before the ship blew even, but I had to wait for the right moment. Sleep, not talk, not move, nothing to waste body water, so I could talk when the time came. Now it's here. Now is the time. You feel it, don't you? Listen to me now.' Kruger's clear, light voice babbled like water running over stones. He stepped up on the stern grating and looked down at the six men frozen into a tableau around the engine. Kinross noted that his sparse white hair lay smooth and saw a hint of set muscles under the fat face.

'I'll tell you a true story so you can understand easy,' Kruger continued. 'Long time ago, long ago, in the Tibesti highlands of Africa, some soldiers were lost and dying of thirst, like us now. They went up a valley, a dry wash with bones on the ground, to two big rocks like pillars side by side. They did something there, and when they went between the two big rocks they were in a different world with green trees and running water. All of them lived and afterwards some of them came back.'

'I heard that story before, somewhere,' Kinross said.

Fay jerked towards him. 'A lie, Kinross! You're welshing! Kruger, it's a stall!'

'I didn't believe the story,' Kinross said mildly. 'I don't believe it now.'

'I do believe it,' Kruger said sharply. 'I *know* it's true. I've been there. I've looked into that world. We can do just what those soldiers did.'

'Bilge, Kruger!' Garcia growled. 'How could there be such a world? How could you get in it?'

'I didn't get in, Garcia. I could see and hear, but when I walked into it everything faded around me.'

'Then what good—'

'Wait. Let me finish. I lacked something we have here. I was alone, not half dead with thirst, and I couldn't all the way believe what I saw and heard.'

'So what does—'

'Wait. Hear me out. Believe me, Garcia, all of you. There are seven of us here and no other humans in a thousand miles. Our need is more than we can stand. We can believe. We must believe or die. Trust me. I know.'

The Mexican scratched the black stubble along his heavy jaw. 'Kruger, I think you're crazy as Whelan,' he said slowly.

'Whelan wasn't crazy,' Kruger said. 'He was just a kid and couldn't wait. He saw a green meadow. Believe me now, all of you, if we all had seen that meadow *at the same time Whelan saw it* we would be walking in it right this minute!'

'Yah, like Whelen now is walking,' Kerbeck put in.

'We *killed* Whelan, do you understand? We killed him because we couldn't believe what he saw and so it wasn't true.' The light, bubbling voice splashed with vehemence.

'I think I get you, Kruger,' Garcia said slowly.

'I don't,' Kinross said, 'unless you want us all to die in a mass hallucination.'

'I want us to *live* in a mass hallucination. We can. We must or die. Believe me. I *know* this.'

'Then you mean go out in a happy dream, not knowing when the end comes?'

'Damn you, Kinross, you've got a little education. That's why it's so hard for you to understand. But let me tell you, this world, this Indian Ocean, is a hallucination too. The whole human race has been a million years building it up, training itself to see and believe, making the world strong enough to stand any kind of shock. It's like a dream we can't wake up from. But believe me, Kinross, you *can* wake up from this nightmare. Trust me. I know the way.'

Kinross thought, 'I'm a fool to argue. It's a delay for me, in any case. But maybe ... maybe...' Aloud he said, 'What you say ... Yes, I know the thought ... but all anyone can do is talk about it. There's no way to *act* on it.'

'The more word-juggling the less action, *that's* why! But we can act, like the soldiers of Tibesti.'

'A myth. A romantic legend.'

'A true story. I've been there, seen, heard. I know. It was long ago, before the Romans, when the web of the world was not so closely woven as now. There were fewer men like you in the world then, Kinross.'

'Kruger,' Kerbeck broke in, 'I heard that story one time myself. You been *sure* now, Kruger?'

'Yes, sure, sure, sure. Kerbeck, I *know* this.'

'I go along, Kruger,' the big Swede said firmly. Garcia said, 'I'm trying, Kruger. Keep talking.'

The clear, light voice resumed its liquid cadence. 'You, Kinross, you're the obstacle. You're the brain, the engineer with a slide rule on the log desk. You're a symbol and you hold back the rest of us. You've got to believe or we'll cut your throat and try with six men. I mean it, Kinross!'

'I want to believe, Kruger. Something in me knows better, but I can feel it slipping. Talk it up. Help me.'

'All right. You know all this already. You're not learning something new but remembering something you were trained to forget. But listen. Reality cracks open sometimes. Indians on vision quest, saints in the Theban desert, martyrs in the flame. Always deprivation, pain long drawn out, like us here, like Whelan yesterday. But always the world heals itself, clanks back together, with the power of the people who will not see, will not believe, because they think they can't believe. Like you helped to kill Whelan yesterday.

'You know something about electricity. Well, it's like a field, strongest where the most people are. No miracles in cities. People hold the world together. They're trained from the cradle up to hold it together. Our language is the skeleton of the world. The words we talk with are bricks and mortar to build a prison in which we turn cannibal and die of thirst. Kinross, do you follow me?'

'Yes, I follow you, but—'

'No buts. Listen. Here were are, 18 south 82 east, seven men in ten million square miles of emptiness. The reality field is weak here. It's a *thin spot* in the world, Kinross, don't you understand? We're at the limit of endurance. We don't care if the public world comes apart in a thousand places if only we can break out of it here, save our lives, drink cool, fresh water...'

Kinross felt a shiver of dread run over him. 'Hold on,' he said. 'I think I do care about the public world coming apart...'

'Hah! You begin to believe!' The clear, smooth voice fountained in triumph. 'It soaks in, under the words and behind the thinking. It scares you. All right. Believe me now, Kinross. I've studied this for half my life. We will not harm the public world when we steal ourselves from it. We will leave a little opening, as in the Tibesti, but who will ever find it?'

The old Portygee waved his skinny arms and croaked. Then he found his voice and said, 'I know the story of Tibesti, Kruger. My fathers have lived in Mogador for six hundred years. It is a Berber story and it is unholy.'

'But true, Silva,' Kruger said softly. 'That's all we care about. We all know it's true.'

'You want a black miracle, Kruger. God will not let you do it. We will lose our souls.'

'We will take personal possession of our souls, Silva. That's what I've been telling Kinross. God is spread pretty thin at 18 south 82 east.'

'No, no,' the old man wailed. 'It is better we pray for a white miracle, a ship, rain to fall...'

'Whatever lets me live is a white miracle,' Garcia said explosively. 'Kruger's right, Silva. I been sabotaging every prayer you made the last four days just by being here. It's the only way for us, Silva.'

'You hear, Kinross?' Kruger asked. 'They believe. They're ready. They can't wait on you much longer.'

'I believe,' Kinross said, swallowing painfully, 'but I have to know *how*. Okay, black magic, but what words, what thoughts, what acts?'

'No words. No thoughts. They are walls to break through. One only act. An unnameable, unthinkable act. I know what bothers you, Kinross. Listen now. I mean group hypnosis, a shared hallucination, something done every day somewhere in the world. But here there is a thin spot. Here there is no mass of people to keep the public world intact. Our hallucination will become the public world to us, with water and fruit and grass. We've been feeling it for days, all around us, waiting for us ...'

The men around Kinross murmured and snuffled. An enormous excitement began to stir in him.

'I believe, Kruger. I feel it now. But how do you know what kind of world ... ?'

'Damn it, Kinross, it's not a pre-existent world. It's only there potentially. We'll make it up as we go along, put in what we want ... a Fiddler's Green.'

'Yah,' said Kerbeck. 'Fiddler's Green. I hear about that too. Hurry up, Kinross.'

'I'm ready,' Kinross said. 'For sure, I'm ready.'

'All right,' Kruger said. 'Now we cross over, to our own world and the fresh, cold water. All of you lie down, stretch out best way you can, like you wanted to rest.'

Kinross lay flat in the after compartment, beside Kerbeck. Kruger looked down at them with his moon face that now seemed hewn of granite. He swayed against the taffrail to the regular pitch and dip of the boat.

'Rest,' he said. 'Don't try, don't strain, or you'll miss it. You, Kinross, don't try to watch yourself. Rest. Don't think. Let your bellies sag and your fingers come apart ...

'Your bodies are heavy, too heavy for you. You are sinking flat against the soft wood. You are letting go, sagging down ...'

Kinross felt the languor and the heaviness. Kruger's voice sounded more distant but still clear, liquid, never-stopping.

'... resting now. Pain is going. Fear is going ... further away ... happy ... sure of things ... you believe me because I know ... you trust me because I know.'

Kinross felt a mouth twitch and it was his own. The inert, heavy body was somehow his own also. There was a singsong rise and fall, like the swells, in Kruger's pattering, babbling voice.

'... resting ... so-o-o relaxed ... can't blink your eyes ... try ... no matter how hard you try.'

Kinross felt a tingling in the hands and feet of the body that could not blink its eyes. But of course ...

'... jaws are stuck ... try hard as you can ... can't open ... hand coming up ... up and up and up ... as a feather ... up and up ... try hard as you can ... KINROSS, try to put your hand down!'

The hand floated in Kinross's field of view. It had something to do with him. He willed it to drop but it would not obey. His vision was pulsating to the rhythm of the swells and the fading in and out of Kruger's voice. First he saw Kruger far off but clear and distinct, like through the wrong way of a telescope, and the voice was clear, burbling, like water falling down rocks. Then the fat man rushed closer and closer, looming larger and larger, becoming more hazy and indistinct as he filled the sky, and the voice faded out. Then the back swing ...

'... hands going down ... relaxed on the soft, restful wood ... all relaxed ... almost ready now ... stay relaxed until I give you the signal ... HEAR THIS NOW: for the signal I will clap my hands twice and say, "Act". You will know what to do and all together you will do it ... take me with you ... each one, reach out a hand and take me along ... blind where you see, deaf where you hear ... must not fail to take me ... REMEMBER THAT.

'... sea is gone, sky is gone, nothing here but the boat and a grey mist. KINROSS, what do you see?'

Grey mist swirling, black boat, no colour, no detail, a sketch in a dream ... no motion ... no more pulsation of things ... the endless plash and murmur of the voice, and then another voice, 'I see grey mist all around.'

'Grey mist all around, and in the mist now one thing. One thing you see. Silva, what do you see?'

'A face. I see a face.'

'Fay, you see the face. Describe the face.'

'A giant's face. Bigger than the boat. It is worried and stern.'

'Kerbeck, you see the face. How is it shaped?'

'Round and fat. A leedle fuzz of beard there is.'

'Garcia, you see the face. Tell us the colours.'

'Eyes blue. Hair almost white. Skin smooth and white. Lips thin and red.'

'KINROSS, you see the face. Describe it in detail.'

'Thin eyebrows, high arched, white against white. Broad forehead. Bulging cheeks. Flat nose, large, flaring nostrils. Wide mouth, thin lips.'

'Bo Bo, you see the face. Who is it, Bo Bo? Tell us who it is.'

'It is you, Boss Kruger.'

'Yes,' said the Face, the great lips moving. 'Now you are ready. Now you are close. Remember the signal. You have let go of yourselves by giving me control. Now I will do for you what no man can do for himself: I will set you free. Remember the signal. Remember your orders.

'You are thirsty. Thirst claws in your throats, tears at your guts. You have to drink. You don't care, don't think. You would drink the blood of your children and of your fathers and not care. Water, cold, wet, splashing water, rivers of water, all around you, waiting for you, green trees and grass and water.

'You already know how to get to it. You always knew, from before time you knew, and now you remember and you are ready for the signal. All together and take me with you. You know what to do. Not in words, not in thoughts, not in pictures, deeper, older, far underneath those, you knew. Before the word, before the thought, there was the act.'

The great mouth gaped on the final word and green light flashed in its inner darkness. The mists swirled closer and Kinross floated there on an intolerable needlepoint of thirst. Great eyes blue-blazing, with dreadful intensity, the Face spoke again:

'IN THE BEGINNING IS THE ACT!'

It shouted the last word tremendously. There was a sharp double clap of thunder and green lightnings played in the cavernous mouth which yawned wide on the word until it filled the field of vision. The green lightnings firmed into trees, mossy rocks, a brawling stream ... Kinross tugged the heavy body after him by one arm, splash, splash, in the cold, clear water.

*

Kinross drank greedily. The coolness flowed into him and out along his arteries and the fire died. He could see the others kneeling in or beside the clear stream running smoothly over rounded pebbles and white sand. Then a great weariness came over him. He drank again briefly, lay down on the smooth turf beside the stream and slept.

When he awoke, Garcia was sitting beside him eating bananas and offered him some. Kinross looked around while he was eating. Level ground extended perhaps ten yards on either side of the little stream; then convexly curved banks rose abruptly for a hundred feet. In the diffuse, watery light the land was green with grass and the darker green of trees and bushes. The colours were flat and homogeneous. There were no random irregularities on the land such as gullies or rock outcrops. The trees were blurred masses never quite in direct view. The grass was blurred and vague. It was like the time he had had his eyes dilated for refraction. But he could see Garcia plainly enough.

Kinross shook his head and blinked. Garcia chuckled.

'Don't let it bother you,' he said. 'Why be curious?'

'Can't help it, I guess,' Kinross replied. Then he spied Kruger's supine form to his left and said, 'Let's wake Kruger.'

'Tried it already,' the Mexican said. 'He ain't dead and he ain't alive. Go see what you think.'

Kinross felt a pang of alarm. Kruger was needed here. He rose, walked over and examined the body. It was warm and pliant but unresponsive. He shook his head again.

Curses broke out behind the indefinite shrubbery on the bank across the stream. Fay's voice. Then the little man came into view beside the huge Negro. They had papayas and guavas.

'Kruger still asleep?' Fay asked. 'Damn him and his world. Everything I pick in it is full of worm-holes and rotten spots.'

'Try some of my bananas here,' Garcia said. Fay ate one and muttered reluctant gratification.

'We've got to do something about Kruger,' Kinross said. 'Let's have a conference.'

'Silva! Kerbeck! Come in!' the Mexican shouted.

The two came down the bank. Kerbeck was eating a large turnip with the aid of his belt knife. Silva fingered his rosary.

'Kruger's in a kind of trance, I think,' Kinross said. 'We'll have to build a shelter for him.'

'There won't be any weather here,' Silva said. 'No day, no night, no shadows. This place is unholy. It isn't real.'

'Nonsense,' Kinross objected. 'It's real enough.' He kicked at the turf, without leaving any mark on it.

'No!' Silva cried. 'Nothing's really here. I can't get close to a tree trunk. They slide away from me.' Kerbeck and Fay mumbled in agreement.

'Let's catch Silva a tree,' Garcia said with a laugh. 'That little one over there. Spread out in a circle around it and keep looking at it so it can't get away.'

Kinross suspected from their expressions that the others shared his own fearful excitement, his sense of the forbidden. All but the mocking Garcia. They surrounded the tree and Kinross could see Kerbeck beyond it well enough, but the smooth, green trunk did seem to slide out of the way of a focused glance.

'We got it for you, Silva,' Garcia said. 'Go in now. Take hold of it and smell it.'

Silva approached the tree gingerly. His wrinkled old face had a wary look and his lips were moving. 'You're not me, tree,' he said softly. 'You've got to be yourself by yourself. You're too smooth and too green.'

Suddenly the old man embraced the trunk and held his face a foot away, peering intently. His voice rose higher. 'Show me spots and cracks and dents and rough places and bumps...'

Fear thrilled Kinross. He heard a far-off roaring noise and the luminous overcast descended in grey swirls. The light dimmed and the flat greens of the landscape turned greyish.

'Silva, stop it!' he shouted.

'Knock it off, Silva!' cried the Mexican.

'...show me whiskers and spines and wrinkles and lines and pits...' Silva's voice, unheeding, rose higher in pitch.

The mists swirled closer. There came a light, slapping, rustling sound. Then a voice spoke, clear and silvery, out of the air above them.

'Silva! Stop that, Silva, or I'll blind you!'

'Unholy!' Silva shrieked. 'I will look *through* you!'

'Silva! Be blind!' commanded the silvery voice. It seemed almost to sing the words.

Silva choked off and stood erect. Then he clapped his hands to his eyes and screamed, 'I'm blind. Shipmates, it's dark! Isn't it dark? The sun went out.'

Kinross, trembling, walked over to Silva as the mists dispersed again.

'Easy, Silva. You'll be all right soon,' he comforted the sobbing old man.

'That voice,' Garcia said softly. 'I know that voice.'

'Yes,' said Bo Bo. 'It was Boss Kruger.'

Okay, Kinross and Garcia agreed, not looking closely at anything. The awareness of the others seemed already so naturally unfocused that they could hardly understand the meaning of the taboo. Kinross did not try to explain. Fay proposed that he stay to look after Silva and Kruger, provided that the others would bring food, since all that he picked for himself was inedible.

'Kinross, let's go for a walk,' Garcia said. 'You haven't looked around yet.'

They walked downstream. 'What happened just now?' Garcia asked.

'I don't know,' Kinross said. 'It was Kruger's voice, all right. Maybe we're really still back in that boat and Kruger is making us dream this.'

'If that's so, I don't want to come out of it,' the Mexican said feelingly, 'but I don't think so. *I'm* real, if this world isn't. When I pinch myself it hurts. My insides work.'

'Me too. But I could sure smell salt water and diesel oil for a few seconds there. Silva almost made us slip back.'

'Kruger was right, I guess,' the Mexican said slowly, 'but it's tough on poor old Silva.'

They walked on in silence beside the rippling stream. Then Kinross said, 'I've got a hankering for apples. Wonder if there are any here?'

'Sure,' said Garcia, 'just over here.' He crossed the stream and pointed out apples on a low-hanging bough. They were large, bright red and without blemish. Kinross ate several with relish before he noticed that they had no seeds and remarked on it to the Mexican.

'Watch it,' warned Garcia. 'No looking close.'

'Well, they taste good.' Kinross said.

'I'll tell you something,' the Mexican said abruptly. 'There's only one tree here. You find it wherever you look for it and it's always got what you want growing on it. I found that out while you were asleep. I experimented.'

Kinross felt the strange dread run over him gently. 'That might be dangerous,' he warned.

'I didn't try to make it be two trees,' the Mexican assured him. 'Something already told me I shouldn't look too close.

'There's something else, too,' Garcia said, when Kinross did not answer. 'I'll let you find out for yourself. Let's climb this bank and see what's on top.'

'Good idea,' Kinross agreed, leading off.

The bank was steeply convex, smooth and regular. Kinross climbed at an angle in order to have a gentler grade and suddenly realized that he was nearly down to the stream again. He swore mildly at his inattention and turned back up the slope, more directly this time. After a few minutes he looked back to see how far down the stream was and realized with a shock that he was really looking up the bank. He looked in front of him again and the floodplain of the little stream was almost at his feet. He could not remember which way he had been going and panic fingered at him.

'Give up,' Garcia said. 'Do you feel it now?'

'I feel something, but what it is...'

'Feel *lost*, maybe?' the Mexican asked.

'No, not lost. Camp, or anyway Kruger, is that way.' Kinross pointed upstream.

'Sure it isn't downstream?'

'Sure as sure,' Kinross insisted.

'Well, go on back and I'll meet you there,' the Mexican said, starting off downstream. 'Look for landmarks on the way,' he called over his shoulder.

Kinross didn't see any landmarks. Nothing stood out in any large, general way. As he approached the group around Kruger's body he saw Garcia coming along the bank from the opposite direction.

'Garcia, does this damn creek run in a circle?' he called in surprise.

'No,' said the Mexican. 'You feel it now, don't you? This world is all one place and you can't cut it any finer. Every time you go up the bank it leads you down to the streambed. Whichever way you walk along the stream, you come to Kruger.'

*

Kinross woke up to see Kerbeck splashing water over his head in the stream. Garcia was sleeping nearby and Kinross woke him.

'What'll we eat this morning?' he asked. 'Papayas, d'ye think?'

'Bacon and eggs,' the Mexican yawned. 'Let's find a bacon-and-egg tree.'

'Don't joke,' Kinross said. 'Kruger won't like it.'

'Oh well, papayas,' Garcia said. He walked down to the stream and splashed water in his face. Then the two men walked up the little valley.

'What do you mean, "this morning"?' Garcia asked suddenly. 'I don't remember any night.'

*

The night was pitch black. 'Kinross,' Garcia called out of the blackness.

'Yes?'

'Remember how it got suddenly dark just now?'

'Yes, but it was a long while back.'

'Bet you won't remember it in the morning.'

'Will there be a morning?' Kinross asked. 'I've been awake forever.' Sleep was a defence.

*

'Wake up, Kinross,' Garcia said, shaking him, 'It's a fine morning to gather papayas.'

'Is it a morning?' Kinross asked. 'I don't remember any night.'

'We gotta talk,' the Mexican grunted. 'Unless we want to sing to ourselves like Kerbeck or moan and cry like Silva over there.'

'Silva? I thought that was the wind.'

'No wind in this world, Kinross.'

*

Kinross bit into a papaya pulp. 'How long have we been here, do you think?' he asked Garcia.

'It's been a while.'

'I can't remember any whole day. Silva was blinded. Was that yesterday? Kerbeck stopped talking and started singing. Was that yesterday?'

'I don't know,' the Mexican said. 'It seems like everything happened yesterday. My beard grew half an inch yesterday.'

Kinross rubbed his own jaw. The brown whiskers were long enough to lie flat and springy.

*

He was walking alone when a whisper came from just behind his head. 'Kinross, this is Kruger. Come and talk to me.'

Kinross whirled to face nothing. 'Where?' he whispered.

'Just start walking,' came the reply, still from behind.

Kinross started up the bank. He climbed steadily, remembering vaguely a previous attempt at doing so, and suddenly looked back. The stream was far below, lost under the convex curve of the bank that was really a valley wall. Miles across the valley was the other wall, curving up in counter-symmetry to the slope he was climbing. He pressed on, wondering, to come out on a height of land like a continental divide. Smooth, sweeping curves fell off enormously on either hand into hazy obscurity.

He walked along it to the right. It had the same terrain of vague grass and indefinite shrubs and trees, flat shades of green with nothing standing out. After a while he saw a gently rounded height rising to his left, but the whisper directed him down a long gentle slope to his right and then up a shorter, steeper slope to a high plain. There was a vast curve to it, almost too great to sense, but the horizon on the left seemed lower than that on the right. He walked on steadily.

Kinross seemed tireless to himself. He did not know how long he had been walking. He climbed another abrupt slope and a series of shallow but enormous transverse swales replaced the rounded plain. The land still curved downward to the left. Far ahead was a clear mountain shape.

It, too, was green. He started up a concave slope which turned steeply convex so that he seemed to be defying gravity as he climbed it. Then the slope levelled off considerably and he was approaching a wall of dark forest beyond which a reddish-black rock pinnacle soared into the sky.

He pushed into the forest, to find it only a half-mile belt of woods which gave way to a desert. This was a dull red, gently rising plain over which were scattered huge reddish boulders many times higher than his head. He picked his way between them over ground which seemed hot and vibrating until he came to the base of the rock pinnacle. As he neared it a pattern of intersecting curves on top indicated that it was cratered.

It was a vertical climb, but Kinross made it with the same inexplicable ease as the earlier ones. He descended a little way into the crater and said, 'Here I am, Kruger.'

Kruger's natural voice spoke out of the air from a point directly ahead. 'Sit down, Kinross. Tell me what you think.'

Kinross sat crosslegged on the rough rock surface. 'I think you're running this show, Kruger,' he said. 'I think maybe you saved my life. Past that, I don't know what to think.'

'You're curious about me, aren't you? Well, so am I. Partly I make up the rules and partly I discover them. This is a very primitive world, Kinross.'

'It's prehuman,' Kinross said. 'You took us deep.'

'Had to, for people like us.'

'You're just a voice in the air to me,' Kinross said. 'How do you experience yourself?'

'I have a body, but I suppose it's a private hallucination. I can't animate my real body. It must be some result of my not having been in deep trance when we crossed over.'

'Is that good or bad for you?'

'Depends. I have unique powers but also special responsibilities. For instance, I am forced to animate this world and my capacity is limited. That's the reason for the taboo on looking closely or trying to use things.'

'Oh. Silva then ... can you restore his sight?'

'Yes, his blindness is purely functional. But I won't. He'd

destroy us all. He'd look and look until our world fell apart. He gave me a bad time, Kinross.'

'I was scared too. Tell me, what would have happened if—?'

'Back in the boat, perhaps. Or some kind of limbo.'

'Is your existence purely mental now, Kruger?'

'No. I told you, I have a hallucinated body which seems perfectly real to me. But it cannot use the substance of this world the way you and the others do. Kinross, I still have the same thirst I had when we came over. It is like—what you remember. I can't quench it and I can't endure it. This world is a kind of hell to me...'

'Holy Moses, Kruger! That's too bad. Can we do anything?'

'I have one hope. It's why I brought you here.'

'Tell me.'

'I want to put you into still deeper hypnosis, deep as man can go. I want to set up such a deep rapport between us that I will share with you the animation of your body and you will share with me the animation of this world. Then I will be able to eat and drink.'

'Granting it's possible, how would that seem to me?'

'You mean animating the world? I can't describe it to you. A joy beyond words.'

'No, I mean you in my body. How do you know I won't have your thirst then? Which of us would be dominant?'

'We could quench the thirst, that's the point. I would grant you dominance in the body and retain my dominance in the world.'

Kinross tugged at his shaggy brown hair. 'I don't know,' he said slowly. 'You scare me, Kruger. Why *me?*'

'Because of your mind, Kinross. You're an engineer. We must build natural law into this world if I am ever to have rest. I need intimate access to your world-picture so that it can inform this world.'

'Why can't I help you just as I am?'

'You can, but not enough. I need to superimpose your world-picture on mine in complete interaction.'

Decision welled up in Kinross. 'No,' he said. 'Take one of the others. Except for Garcia and maybe Silva they hardly seem to know they're alive, but they eat and drink.'

'I've taken a large part of them into the world already, and something of you and Garcia too. But I want you intact, as a unity.'

'No.'

'Think of the power and the joy. It is indescribable, Kinross.'

'No.'

'Think of what you can lose. I can blind you, paralyse you.'

'I'll grant that. But you won't. In a way I can't explain I know you need us, Kruger. You need our eyes and ears and our understanding minds in order to see and appreciate this world of yours. Your sight dimmed when you blinded Silva.'

'That isn't wholly true. I needed you absolutely in order to get across, in order to form this world, but not now.'

'I'll gamble you're lying, Kruger. You don't have a large enough population to afford playing tyrant.'

'Don't underestimate me, Kinross. You don't know me and you never can. I have a fierce will in this matter that must not be denied. From childhood on I have worked toward this culmination with absolute ruthlessness. I deliberately did not send a distress message from the *Ixion* because I wanted the chance I got. Does that impress you?'

'Not in your favour, Kruger. So little Ratface was right.'

'I don't want your favour or your pity, Kinross. I want your conviction that you cannot stand out against me. I'll tell you more. I planted the bomb in the *Ixion*'s cargo hold. I dumped the food and water out of the launch. I ran down the battery and jammed the fuel pump. I timed the explosion so that you would be just coming off watch. That convinces you. Now you know that you cannot stand out against such a will as mine.'

Kinross stood up and squinted his brown eyes into the emptiness before him. 'I'm convinced that you made your own world but now you can't get all the way into it. I'm convinced that you should not. Kruger, to hell with you.'

'It is my world and I'll come all the way into it in spite of you,' Kruger said. 'Look at me!' On the command the voice rang out strong and silvery, a great singing.

'You're not there,' Kinross said, standing up.

'Yes I am here. Look at me.'

The air before Kinross became half visible, a ghostly streaming upward.

'Look at me!' the chiming, silvery voice repeated.

There came a sound like tearing silk. The hair stood up on Kinross's neck and a coldness raced over his skin. The streaming air thickened and eddied, became a surface whorled and contoured in a third dimension, became vibrantly alive, became the shape of a great face.

Kinross, look at me!' the Face commanded in a voice like great bells.

Kinross took a deep breath. 'I learn my lesons well, Kruger,' he said in a trembling voice. 'You're not there. I don't see you.'

He walked directly into the Face and through it, feeling an electric thrill in his cringing flesh as he did so. Then he was clambering down the sheer face of the pinnacle.

As Kinross crossed the high plain on his way back, rain began to fall from the overcast. Gusts of wind buffeted him. There was no surface run-off of the rain and no clear effect of the wind in the indefinite trees and shrubbery. 'Kruger's learning,' Kinross said to himself. The darkness came suddenly and he lay down and slept. When he awoke he was back beside the little stream and Garcia told him he had been gone four days.

*

'Four days?' Kinross asked in surprise. 'Doesn't everything still happen yesterday?'

'Not any more,' the Mexican said. 'Where in hell have you been?'

'Outside somehow, arguing with Kruger,' Kinross said, looking around. 'Damn it this place feels different. And where's Kruger's body and the others?'

'It is different,' Garcia said. 'I'll tell you. First, Fay found a cave ...'

The cave was the source of the stream, which now ran out of it, Garcia explained. Fay and Bo Bo had carried Kruger's body into it and now spent most of their time in there. Fay claimed that Kruger awoke at intervals to eat and drink and that he made Fay his spokesman. Fay and Bo Bo piled up a cairn of rocks before the cave mouth and had commanded Kerbeck and Garcia to bring fruit and place it there every morning. Silva now sat beside the cairn, rocking and wailing as before.

'I couldn't make Kerbeck understand,' Garcia added. 'He roams the hillsides now like a wild man. So I've been supplying them by myself.'

'The place is bigger,' Kinross commented. The valley floor extended now for several hundred yards on either side of the little stream and the walls rose hundreds of feet. The oppressive regularity of outline was relieved by a hint of weather sculpturing and meaningful groupings of plant life.

'Space is nailed down better too,' Garcia. 'There are all kinds of trees now that stay put and can be looked at.' He slapped at a fly buzzing around his head.

'Hello!' Kinross exclaimed. 'Insects!'

'Yes,' Garcia agreed sourly. 'Little animals in the brush, too. Rats and lizards, I think. And I got rained on once. It ain't all good, Kinross.'

'Let's go see that cave,' Kinross proposed. 'I'll tell you what happened to me on the way.'

They walked half a mile upstream. The valley narrowed and its walls became more vertical. A tangled growth of dark timber trees filled it. The diffuse light from the permanently overcast sky scarcely penetrated its gloom. Then they came into a clearing perhaps a hundred yards across and Kinross could see the darkly wooded slopes rising steeply on three sides. Directly ahead was the cave.

Two relatively narrow basaltic dikes slanted up the slope for more than a hundred feet, coming together at the top to form an inverted V. The stream ran out of the cavernous darkness at its base, bisected the clearing and lost itself in the dark wood. Near where the stream emerged, Kinross could see the cairn like a low stone platform about ten feet across and he could see and hear Silva, who sat wailing beside it.

'I can't talk to Silva no more than Kerbeck,' Garcia said. 'Silva thinks I'm a devil.'

They walked across the clearing. The giant Bo Bo came out of the cave to meet them.

'You have not brought fruit,' he said, in words that Kinross knew were never his own. 'Go away and return with fruit.'

'Okay, Kruger,' Kinross said. 'That much I'll do for you.'

*

Days passed. To Kinross they seemed interminable, yet curiously void of remembered activity. He and Garcia tried marking off time with stones from the creek, but overnight the stones disappeared. So did banana peels and papaya rinds. The land would not hold a mark. The two men wrangled over what had happened in the preceding days and at last Kinross said, 'It's just like before, only now everything happened last week.'

'Then my beard grew an inch last week,' said Garcia, stroking its blue-blackness. Kinross's beard was crinkled and reddish and more than an inch long.

'What's the end of this?' the Mexican asked once. 'Do we just go on in this two-mile-across world forever?'

'I expect we'll get old and die,' Kinross said.

'I ain't so sure even of that,' Garcia said. 'I feel like I'm getting younger. I want a steak and a bottle of beer and a woman.'

'So do I,' Kinross agreed, 'but this is still better than the boat.'

'Yes,' Garcia said feelingly. 'Give Kruger that much, even if he did set the whole thing up.'

'I think Kruger is a lot less happy than we are,' Kinross said.

'Nobody's happy but Kerbeck,' Garcia growled.

They saw Kerbeck often as they gathered fruit or tramped the confines of the little valley seeking relief of boredom. The giant Swede ranged through the land like an elemental spirit. He wore the remnants of his khaki trousers and singlet, and his yellow hair and red beard were long and tangled. He seemed to recognize Garcia and Kinross, but made only humming noises in response to their words.

*

Kinross often felt that it was the unrelieved blackness of the nights which oppressed him most. He wanted stars and a moon. One night he awoke feeling uneasy and saw a scattering of stars in the sky, strangely constellated. He moved to wake Garcia but sleep overcame him again and he dreamed for the first time he could remember in that world. He was back on the rock pinnacle in the desert talking to Kruger. Kruger was wearing Fay's body and he was worried.

'Something's happened, Kinross,' he said. 'There are stars and I didn't shape them; I couldn't. This world has suddenly received a great increase in animation and not all of it is under my control.'

'What can I do about it? Or care?'

'You care, all right. We're in this world together, like in a lifeboat, Kinross. And I'm scared now. There's an alien presence, perhaps a number of them, seeking our world. They may be hostile.'

'I doubt it, if they bring stars,' Kinross said. 'Where are they?'

'I don't know. Wandering outside of our space here, looking for us, I suppose. I want you and Garcia to go and find them.'

'Why can't you do that?'

'Your guess was partly right, Kinross. I have my limits and my need for men like you and Garcia. I'm asking, not commanding. We're still in the same boat, remember.'

'Yes. Okay, I'll go. But how ... ?'

'Just start walking. I'll let you through the re-entry barrier again.'

Kinross awoke with a start. The stars were still in the sky and a crescent moon hung above the horizon across the little stream. Garcia snored nearby.

'Wake up!' Kinross said, shaking him. The Mexican snorted and sat up.

'*Madre de Dios!*' he gasped. 'Stars and a moon! Kinross, are we back ... ?'

'No,' Kinross said. 'Let's go hunting. I've just been talking to Kruger.'

'Hunting? At night? Hunting what?'

'Maybe what made the stars. How do I know? Come on, Garcia, my feet are burning.'

Kinross strode off, leaping the creek and heading directly towards the crescent moon. The Mexican stumbled after him muttering in Spanish.

*

Once more Kinross reached the height of land, and the moon, fuller now, hung above the horizon on the right, in the same direction he had gone before. He walked briskly, the Mexican following in silence. Once Garcia exclaimed and pointed down to the right. Kinross looked and saw the cave mouth far below, the dwarfed clearing and the mighty slope curving convexly up from it to his present level. The moonlight touched the dark treetops with silver.

As they walked Kinross told Garcia about his dream. The Mexican did not doubt that it was genuine. Kinross warned him about the peculiar timelessness of experience outside the re-entry barrier. 'It's like everything happened two minutes ago,' he said.

'Yes,' said Garcia. 'Look at that moon now, three-quarters full. Maybe we've been walking for a month.'

'Or a minute,' Kinross said.

It was not to be the same trip as before. Once on the high, gently curving plain he remembered, he found they were bearing sharply to the right, going up a gentle rise. Then the land pitched the other way and they began crossing shallow ravines with running water in their bottoms. The land grew rougher and the ravines deeper until, crossing one of them, Kinross saw that it bore directly for the moon. He continued down the stream bed in ankle-deep water instead of climbing out.

The banks were wet, dark stone and became steeper and higher as they went. The stream narrowed and became knee-deep and the current tugged fiercely at them, forcing them to cling to the stones to maintain their footing. The sharp V of the ravine ahead almost cradled the full moon and Kinross could hear the distant roar of falling water.

'Looks rough up ahead, Garcia,' he called to the Mexican ten feet behind him. 'Watch it.'

He moved ahead another hundred yards towards the increasing noise and edged around a rock shoulder against which the water swirled angrily. The force of the current quickened suddenly, almost snatching his legs from under him, so that he flattened himself against the rock and called a warning back to Garcia.

Over the glassily smooth, veined lip of the waterfall twenty feet in front of him, Kinross looked into a vast pit, steeply conical and many miles across. It was beaded around the rim and threaded down the sides with falling water and whispered enormously across the distance. The full moon riding directly above washed the whole with silver. At the bottom of the pit was another moon which, Kinross thought fleetingly, must be a reflecting pond or lake.

Garcia called from behind. 'What do you see, Kinross? Why have you stopped?'

'I see one more step and death, I think,' Kinross called back. 'It's a waterfall. We'll have to climb the bank here, if we possibly can.'

He made no move to return, but stared down into the pit. Abruptly the urge came to him to surrender, to let the water carry him over the brink. It was sudden and overpowering, almost sexual, a savage assault on his spirit. He clung desperately to the rock face and muttered a prayer under his breath, 'Mother of God, spare me now.'

The compulsion, still powerful, withdrew a little distance. 'Garcia,' he called, 'start climbing, in the name of God. Keep talking to me.'

'There's a ledge back here, slanting up,' Garcia said from above. 'Come back under me and I'll give you a hand up.'

Kinross edged back around the rock shoulder and scrambled up to join Garcia. The Mexican led the way up the narrow ledge.

'There's something up ahead that will take your breath away,' Kinross warned him. 'A pit. Wait till you see it. And when you do, hang on to yourself.'

Garcia grunted and kept climbing. The ledge petered out and the way became more difficult and dangerous. Then they were standing on a rocky headland falling steeply on three sides into the great pit that was all around them.

'*Madre de Dios!*' breathed Garcia. He repeated it several times, otherwise speechless. Both men stood silently, gazing into the pit. Finally Garcia raised a hand and whispered, 'Listen!'

Kinross listened. He heard a crackling of brush and a rattling of dislodged pebbles. It came from the left, seemingly not far off.

'Something's coming up out of the pit,' he whispered.

'What's coming? Kinross, we ain't alone in this world!'

'We've got to go closer,' Kinross said. 'Have to know. Walk easy.'

They stalked the sound, retreating from the headland and skirting the edge of the pit. As they neared the source of the noise, the brush became tangled and waist-high and they made noises of their own, unavoidably. Then all was silent and Kinross feared their quarry was alarmed until he heard a snuffling, whimpering noise that set his nerves still more on edge. They crept closer. Then Garcia grasped his arm and pulled him to a crouch.

Kinross strained his eyes towards where the Mexican was pointing. Suddenly, taking vague form in the pattern of silvery light and shadow, he saw a human figure not fifty feet away. 'We capture him,' he told Garcia in dumb show. The Mexican nodded. Both men rose and rushed headlong.

Kinross's longer legs got him there first. The figure rose and fled a step or two before he brought it down with a flying tackle. A split second later the stocky Mexican added his considerable weight to the tangle of arms and legs and then a despairing, agonized scream arose from the captive. Electric surprise jolted Kinross.

'Let go, Garcia,' he commanded. 'Get up. It's a woman!'

*

She was Mary Chadwick and she had three strong brothers who could clobber any man in Queensland, and Kinross and Garcia were beasts and savages and they were to take her home immediately or it would be the worse for them. Then she clung to Kinross and cried hysterically.

While Kinross tried awkwardly to comfort her, day came, less abruptly than usual but swiftly enough to remind Kinross how unaccountably time still ran. The light was harsh and bright and he saw the disc of the sun for the first time. The familiar overcast was gone, the sky clear and blue. Sight of the two bearded men did not seem to reassure the woman.

She was quite young and dressed for riding, khaki shirt and trousers, with laced boots, outlining a tall and generous figure. Honey-coloured hair hung loose to her shoulders. Her eyes, swollen with crying, were an intense blue verging on violet. Her fair skin was tanned to pale gold and a dusting of freckles lay across the bridge of her strong nose.

She recovered quickly. 'Who are you?' she asked in a clear

but low-pitched voice. 'What is this place? Nothing like it in the Coast Ranges *I* ever heard of.'

The men introduced themselves. Kinross failed completely to make her understand the nature of the world around them.

'Ships? Sailors? What rot!' she exclaimed. 'You say you don't understand it yourselves, so go along with that nonsense. All we need do is walk until we find a track or see smoke or – you know all that.'

'Okay, we're lost then,' Kinross agreed. 'We're somewhere in Australia, I take it?'

'Yes, Queensland, and somewhere on the south fork of the Herbert River. I was riding along and I must have fallen asleep ... where my horse is, I'm sure I have no earthly notion.'

Kinross and Garçia exchanged glances. 'Excuse me, Mary,' the Mexican said, his black eyes blazing with excitement. 'I just have to talk crazy for a minute to my friend here.' Then to Kinross, 'How come? According to the soldiers-of-Tibesti story the gate should be in the Indian Ocean. Has this world got more than one hole in it, you suppose?'

'That's bothering me, too. The way I've always understood it, without ever believing any of it, mind you, the two worlds are not superimposed. They just have that one small area in common, the gate ...'

'Well, if it opens on land ...'

'I know what you're thinking. But we've got to give Kerbeck and Silva a chance. Anyway, those two.' Kinross turned to the girl.

'Mary,' he asked, 'can you remember exactly where in that pit you first found yourself? Did you mark the spot?'

'No, why should I have? I'll not go back down there for all the mad fossickers in the entire North. Take me to your camp or your diggings or whatever. I hope someone there will talk sense to me.'

The Mexican laughed suddenly. 'I just remembered old Bart Garcia, my first ancestor in Mexico, was a prospector too,' he said. 'That was a new world and he had a rough time in it. Lead on, Kinross.'

'All roads lead to Kruger,' said Kinross, striding off.

'All but one,' Garcia corrected, looking back at the great pit, shadowed now by slanting sunlight.

*

The way back was rugged at first, then more gentle. Kinross exclaimed in pleased surprise when a bird fluttered through the brush and Garcia said, 'So that's what I been hearing.' Then Kinross heard it too, a multitudinous chirping and twittering all around them. But the birds, like the indefinite trees and shrubs, were always annoyingly peripheral to direct vision. They were wing flashes, darting colours at the edge of sight.

'Doesn't it bother you, not being able to look at them?' he asked the girl.

'But I can see them,' she said. 'You strange men...'

Keck-keck-keck-kee-RACK! came a noise from the brush and Kinross jumped.

'There!' the girl pointed. 'It's a coachwhip. Can't you see him now?'

Kinross could not. 'There,' she insisted, 'hopping about in the wattle. Just *look*, won't you!'

Garcia saw it first. Finally Kinross believed he saw the small, dark green thrush shape with white throat, long, perky tail and black crest. But he felt uneasily that he was really seeing a verbal description. Keck-keck-keck-kee-RACK! He jumped again and felt foolish.

As they walked, Kinross questioned the girl. She lived on a small cattle station in the mountains south of Cairns with her father and three brothers. She was twenty-four and unmarried, had spent a year at school in Brisbane, didn't like cities. Her brothers worked part-time in the mines. This would be first-rate country for running stock and she couldn't imagine how the land survey had missed it.

'Look at the sun, Kinross,' Garcia said once. 'We're going west. Feels good to be able to say that.'

The sun was low when they reached the height of land above the valley. 'Kruger Valley,' Kinross called it, since the girl demanded a name. The stupendous wooded slope rising on three sides from the cave mouth was touched with a glory by the declining sun and her pose of matter-of-fact assurance broke once more.

'Nothing like that in the Coast Ranges,' she whispered. 'I just know it.'

When they started down the slope west of the forested area, Kinross was impressed too. Trees stood out in view, unique, individual. The coarse grass was plain to see, as well as clumps of flowers in bright colours. Small, brightly varicoloured birds flitted ahead of them and Kinross knew that he was really seeing them. The flat sameness of colour and the smooth regularity of form were gone from the land. Kinross with rising excitement pointed out to Garcia rock outcrops, gullies and patches of erosion-bared earth.

'Something's happened, Garcia,' he said. 'Here, inside the re-entry barrier, the land sticks backward into time now.'

'Looks sure enough real,' the Mexican agreed. 'Wonder if we could light a fire tonight?'

'Yes, and chop trees,' Kinross almost shouted. 'Mary will need a shelter.'

'Of *course* a fire,' the woman said. 'We shall want to roast things, I suppose.'

'Maybe knock down some birds,' Garcia said. 'I'm hungry for meat.'

'No!' the girl cried in outrage. 'You wouldn't dare!'

'Not these pretty little ones,' Garcia hastily assured her. 'What do you call them, anyway?'

'They're pittas,' she said. 'Noisy little paint pots, aren't they? They say, "Walk-to-WORK, walk-to-WORK".'

'That's what we're doing, I guess,' Garcia chuckled.

They picked their way down the fairly steep hillside, Kinross preparing the girl for what she would find down by the stream, when she interrupted him.

'Who are they?' she asked, pointing to the left.

Kinross and Garcia could see nothing. 'What is it you see?' Kinross asked.

'A whole band of blacks, myalls,' she whispered, obviously disturbed. 'On their knees, in the bush.'

'Now I partly see them,' the Mexican said. 'It's worse than the birds were this morning.'

'I can't see a thing,' Kinross complained. 'Only trees and shrubs.'

'Look slantwise,' Garcia urged. 'Let your eyes go slack. Every kid knows how to do that.'

Kinross tried to unfocus his gaze and suddenly he saw them, dozens of them. Dwarfs, black with red eyes. Naked and grotesquely formed, huge hands and feet, knobbed joints, slubber lips, limbs knotted with muscles. They were looking back at him, but without apparent interest. Alarm bit into him.

'My God!' he breathed.

'They're a pack of devils,' Garcia muttered. 'Kinross, what in hell are they?'

'They're blacks,' the girl said. 'Back in the earlies they used to spear white men sometimes in the Coast Ranges, but they're tame enough now. We must just walk by and pretend not to see them. They're supposed to be in the spirit world.'

'They're dwarfs, pygmies,' Kinross objected. 'Do you have pygmies in Queensland?'

'They're on their knees,' she answered sharply, 'hiding from us in one of their spirit places. Come along! Walk by and pretend not to see them.'

'Let's try,' Kinross assented.

They walked on without incident until they reached the valley floor. As they walked along the level, Garcia began looking sharply to left and right.

'Kinross, something's dogging us, slipping through the brush after us on both sides,' he said.

'Those black things?' Kinross asked, stomach muscles knotting.

'No, can't see well, but they're taller and greylike.'

'I can see them,' the girl said. 'They're gins, Binghi women of that mob we passed. They look like ghosts when they smear themselves with wood ashes.'

'What are they after?' Kinross asked, half seeing the elusive shapes in the corner of his eye.

'They want to trail us to our camp so they can steal and beg,' the girl said. 'Mind you send them away straight off when they come in.'

Garcia said, 'They got nice shapes, now that I know they're women. Kinross, can you see them yet?'

'Just partly,' Kinross said.

The flitting shapes left them before they reached the stream. As they stood doubtfully on the bank, distant shouting came from the hillside they had just descended. Kinross saw Kerbeck charging through the scrub, black motes scattering before him.

'God!' he gasped. 'Kerbeck's fighting the black things!'

'Winning, too,' Garcia commented, less perturbed than Kinross. 'Look at 'em run.'

'He shouldn't,' the girl said. 'They'll creep back and spear him tonight. All of us, perhaps.' She shuddered.

Kerbeck came plunging down the hill in great leaps. He crossed the quarter mile of valley floor, in and out of sight, looming up bronzed and gigantic. His floating hair and beard were an aureole in the light of the westering sun. He shouldered Kinross aside and grasped the girl by her upper arms, staring fixedly into her eyes. He was humming and buzzing frantically.

Kinross pulled vainly at one of the great arms, protesting. Then the Swede quieted, releasing the girl, smiling and humming placidly.

'It's all right,' the girl said. 'He wanted to be sure that my eyes had pupils.'

Kinross looked blankly from her blue-violet eyes to the flat blue eyes of the huge Norseman.

'He's been chasing the devil-devils,' she explained. 'He thought I might be one. Their eyes don't have pupils, just black smudges on white eyeballs.' Kerbeck hummed happily. Kinross shook his head.

'She's right, Kinross,' Garcia said. 'I got part of it. It's another one of them things, you got to listen sideways-like.'

'They turn into trees and rocks when he catches them,' the girl added. 'He's been up a gum tree for days about them and he's glad you two are back.'

'Oh lord!' Kinross groaned. 'I feel like a damned infant. So you do agree they're devils now?'

'No more!' she said sharply. 'They're abos on a spirit-land walkabout. The whole push of you are mad as snakes.'

'Let's make a fire,' Kinross said, turning away.

There was plenty of dried grass and fallen branches, unlike before. Garcia had matches, soon had a fire. Kinross borrowed Kerbeck's belt knife to trim poles from the branches the giant

Swede obligingly pulled off the trees, and work on a small hut went forward rapidly. Garcia cut fronds from a palmetto-like tree to weave between the upright poles, and the girl gathered brownish wool from the top of it to make herself a bed. 'Burrawang', she called it. She pronounced the finished effort a passable 'humpy'.

Under the darkness they roasted nubbly breadfruit in the coals and peeled bananas. Kerbeck melted into the night. All ate in silence. Finally the girl said, 'Where are we? Fair truth, now. Where are we?'

'Like I told you this morning —' Kinross began, but she stopped him.

'I know. I believe it has to seem that way to you. But do you know where I am?'

Both men murmured their question.

'In Alcheringa,' she said. 'In the Binghi spirit land. I fell into it somehow, riding through one of the old sacred places. There are picture writings all along the South Herbert. Today, when I saw the abos, I knew...'

'Mary, they *were* dwarfs,' Kinross said. 'They were not human.'

'When the abos go back to the spirit land they are not human either,' she said. 'And at the same time something more than human. I've heard mobs of talk about it. But those gins — they shouldn't be here. Nor I. It's frightful bad luck for a woman to enter the spirit land. When I was a little girl I used to think it blanky unfair.'

'How do the natives get in and out of ... Alcheringa?' Kinross asked with quickened interest.

'They dance and sing their way, paint themselves, use churingas — oh, all sorts of rites,' she said. 'No one must be about, especially no women.'

From the darkness overhead a weird, whistling wail floated down. Both men jumped to their feet.

'Sit down,' the girl bade them. 'At home, on Chadwick Station, I would call that the cry of a stone curlew. They fly about and call in the darkness. The blacks call them the souls of children trying to break out of the spirit world in order to be born. What are they here, I wonder?'

She looked upward. Kinross and Garcia sat down again. Then a slender bird with thin legs and long, curving beak dropped into the firelight to perch on her shoulder.

'Poor little night baby,' the girl addressed it, 'you'll watch over me, won't you?'

She rose abruptly, said goodnight and went into the hut. Kinross looked at Garcia.

'We're responsible for her being here,' he said. 'We've got to get her back to her people.'

'Kruger's responsible,' Garcia said.

'Us too. If Kruger doesn't come talk to me tonight I'm going in the cave in the morning. Will you come along?'

'Sure,' said the Mexican, yawning. 'Pleasant dreams.'

*

Red dawn above the great slope up-valley woke Kinross from a dreamless sleep. He blew an ember into flame and built up the fire. Charred breadfruit rinds littered the ground and he reflected wryly that this world no longer policed itself. He put the rinds into the fire.

Somewhere on the hillside across the stream, Kerbeck shouted and brush crackled. Garcia got up and the woman peeped out of her hut as Kinross stood irresolute. Then Kerbeck came in view. He carried a stalk of yellow bananas over his left shoulder and with his right hand clutched a small man by the neck. He half pushed, half kicked the little man down the slope.

The huge Norseman hummed excitedly as he approached across the level. Suddenly Kinross, still half asleep, heard words in the humming, as he had sometimes heard wind-voices in the singing of telegraph wires when he was a boy on the high plains of Nebraska.

'I catch me a devil,' Kerbeck was saying.

The devil was a swarthy, broad-faced little man dressed in baggy grey woollen garments. His eyes were closed, his face screwed up in fear, and he was gabbling under his breath. Garcia listened, suddenly alert, and then spoke sharply to the man in Spanish. He got a torrent of words in reply.

'He's a Peruvian,' Garcia interpreted. 'He comes from the mountains above Tacna. He's been wandering lost for days. He thinks he's dead and that Kerbeck is the boss devil.'

'Seems to be mutual,' Kinross said. 'Tell him he'll be all right now. I wonder how many more...'

Kerbeck went away, humming and buzzing. The little Peruvian, still badly frightened, crouched beyond the fire and ate bananas with them. Then Kinross, explaining his purpose to the woman, proposed to Garcia that they visit the cave.

'Not empty-handed,' the Mexican reminded him. 'Remember, we got a duty.'

Along the way they gathered guavas and papayas into Kinross's shirt, pushed through the grove and laid the fruits on the stone platform. Silva sat beside it, rocking and wailing almost inaudibly. Kinross patted his shoulder.

'Cheer up, Silva, old man,' he said. 'We're going in to see Kruger now. May have some good news for you.'

'Unholy,' the old man moaned. 'Full of devils. You're a devil.'

The two men walked to the cave mouth and stopped. They looked at each other.

'What are we waiting for?' Garcia asked.

'I don't know. I expected Fay or Bo Bo to be on guard, I guess,' Kinross said. 'Hell with it. In we go.'

The cave pinched sharply in to become a nearly round tunnel about fifteen feet high. The stream splashed along the bottom, forcing them to wade. The water shone with a soft light and moisture oozing through cracks in the black rock made luminous patches here and there on the walls. The rock had the blocky, amorphous look of basalt. The air was cool and utterly still except for the murmur of the stream.

The two men waded in silence for a good way before they heard a clear noise of turbulent water somewhere ahead. Then they came into an indefinitely large chamber with the luminous water cascading broadly down its back wall from a blackness above. Fay and Bo Bo were asleep on rough terraces beside the stream.

'What have you come to tell me, Kinross?' Kruger's voice asked out of the dimness. It seemed to shape the noise of the cascading water into its words.

*

'We found a woman,' Kinross said.

'I know. There are many others, both men and women, still making their way here. I have been greatly strengthened. Have you noticed how the world has firmed up and become extended in time?'

'Yes. But how do these people get here? Is there more than one gate?'

'No. It must have shifted.'

'To where, then? One is from Australia, one from Peru.'

'So?' Surprise rang in the silvery, liquid voice. 'Perhaps it moves then.'

'But Tibesti—'

'They didn't know a rotating earth. The sun of Tibesti goes around a stationary earth. But when we—I—set up a succession of days here I must have put a spin into this world. Perhaps it is slightly out of phase with our old world. The gate would wander...'

'You sound pleased,' Kinross said.

'I am. It takes many people to hold a world in place, Kinross. In a few centuries there may be enough here so that I can really rest. They will breed of course, and they will be long-lived here.'

'How big do you think the gate is?'

'About the size of the boat, I expect. Perhaps an ellipse thirty feet on the major axis.'

'How do people come through, not knowing—?'

'Several ways are possible. Perhaps it sweeps over them at a moment of intense world-loathing, those moments a man can't support beyond a second or two. It snatches them up. Or perhaps daydreamers, with their sense of reality unfocused and their mooring lines to their real world slacked or cast loose. They want only to drift a little way out, but the gate comes by and snatches them. I don't really know, Kinross. Maybe this world is going to be populated by poets and self-haters.'

'But the gate? Can we get through it the other way?'

'Yes. Some of the soldiers of Tibesti came back—or fled back or were driven back—the old tales are conflicting. But anyone passing back through this gate would risk dropping into an ocean. I suspect the gate sweeps the eighteenth parallel, or near it.'

'Kruger, the woman wants to go back. We have to find a way.'

'No. No one may go back. Especially not women.'

'Kruger, we have no right—'

'We do have a right and beyond that a duty. She would not be here if she had not voluntarily, at least for a moment, relinquished or rejected her own world. She belongs to us now, and we need her.'

'Kruger, I may not obey that. I—'

'You must obey. You cannot pass the re-entry barrier without my aid.'

'Let it go, then, for now,' Kinross conceded. 'I have other questions. What are the black dwarfs and pearly-grey women?'

'Nature spirits, I suppose you could call them. I stripped them from Fay and Bo Bo, husked them off by the millions until only a bare core of nothingness was left. What those two are now I couldn't describe to you. But the world is partially self-operating and my load is eased.'

Garcia spoke for the first time. 'Tough on Fay, for all I hated the little rat.'

'Was that what you wanted to do with me?' Kinross asked, shuddering.

'No,' the clear, liquid voice said solemnly, 'you are a different kind of man, Kinross. You could have helped me to bear the load, and perhaps together we could have endured it until the help came that is coming now. Do not wash your hands of Fay and Bo Bo, Kinross.'

'Kruger,' Garcia said hesitantly, 'do you mean that all those devils are really Fay and Bo Bo?'

'Most of them are,' the silvery voice confirmed, 'but many of them are Kerbeck. He is disintegrating without my interference. And some are you, too, Garcia; some are Kinross, the woman, all of you. You are built into this world more than you know.'

'I don't like it,' Garcia said. 'Kruger, I won't give up my devils.'

'You can't help it, Garcia. But you have millions to spare, and besides you don't really lose them, you know. You just spread yourself through the world, in a way. Every time you put a compulsion on this world by expecting something, it costs you a devil or two. Do you understand?'

'No!' the Mexican growled.

'I think you do. If you don't, talk to Kinross later. But it's not so bad, Garcia. When you become a loose cloud of devils, instead of a shiny black stone, you will be a poet or a sylvan god.'

'Kruger,' Kinross broke in, 'do you hold it against me, that I denied you my help that time?'

'Do you hold it against me that I initiated all this by blowing up the *Ixion*?'

'I don't know ... I just don't know ...'

'Nor do I know, Kinross. Perhaps we're even. And I still have need of you.'

'Where is your body, Kruger? Can you animate it yet?'

'It is above the waterfall. I can see dimly now how I will animate it in the distant future and come into this world in a kind of glory. But not yet, not yet ...'

'Your thirst, Kruger. Are you still thirsty?'

'Yes, Kinross. It still tears at me. I don't know how much longer I will have to endure it.'

'Doesn't rapport with Fay – ?'

'No one but you, Kinross. And now not even you. You disobeyed me once.'

'Kruger, I'm sorry. I wish it didn't have to be. May we go now?'

'Yes. Go and serve our world. Try to be content.'

'Let's go, Garcia,' Kinross said, turning. The Mexican set off briskly, leading Kinross. When they were passing through the dark grove Kinross halted.

'Let's sit here and talk about devils for a while, Garcia,' he proposed. 'I'm not ready to face Mary Chadwick just yet.'

*

When the two men returned to the fire, more than a dozen people were standing around it. Several were women. A tall, slender man wearing a leather jacket and grey trousers tucked into heavy boots came out of the group to meet them. He had reddish-blond hair.

'Mr Kinross?' he asked. 'Allow me to introduce myself and to apologize for making free of your fire. My name is Friedrich von Lankenau.'

They shook hands. The newcomer had a sinewy grip in his

long fingers. His face was gaunt and bony, frozen with thin lips and a high, narrow beak of a nose. Kinross stared at him quizzically and deep-set grey eyes looked back at him steadily from under shaggy brows. The thin lips smiled slightly.

'Miss Chadwick tells me that you are Mr Kruger's lieutenant, so to speak,' the man said. 'We are a group gathered together in chance meetings along the way here. We are anxious to learn a rational, physical explanation of what we are experiencing.'

A babble of voices broke from the group. 'Silence!' snapped the tall man. 'If Mr Kinross will explain, you may all listen, you who know English. I will then to the others explain.' The babble stilled.

Kinross told the story of the soldiers of Tibesti and of the sailors of the *Ixion*. He watched Lankenau closely as he spoke. The man never lost the rigid composure of his features, but his eyes blazed and he continually nodded his comprehension. When he finished Kinross checked the renewed babble by setting Garcia to telling the story in Spanish. Then he drew Lankenau to one side.

'Mind telling me where you where when you came through?' he asked.

'I was nearly to the top of Sajama in Bolivia, climbing alone.'

'How about the others?'

'From all over. Brazil, the New Hebrides, Mozambique, Australia, Rhodesia.'

'I guess Kruger's right and the gate does sweep the eighteenth parallel,' Kinross mused.

'We can establish it quite exactly with a little questioning, I have no doubt,' Lankenau said confidently. 'But sooner or later, Mr Kinross, I would like to talk directly to the Herr Kruger if it can be arranged. I am much intrigued—'

'You just go see him, Mr Lankenau. I'm not his secretary. But I can tell you now, he will permit no one to return to the old world.'

'I would not for anything return to the old world!' Lankenau spoke with feeling that broke through his composure.

'From boyhood I knew the story of the soldiers of Tibesti,' he continued. 'As a very young man I sought the gate through

135

all of the Tibesti, and perhaps found the spot, but it did not reveal itself to me as it did for the Herr Kruger. So I sought a gate of my own, on mountaintops in winter, such peaks as Sajama. I am not at all sure that I came through my gate, Mr Kinross, but I am sure that I came to stay.'

'Mary — Miss Chadwick — has somewhat the same notion,' Kinross said. 'I never knew so many people —' His voice trailed off.

'Forgive my outburst,' Lankenau said, composure regained. 'For me this is a lost hope suddenly realized, and I am a bit overcome. If you will excuse me, I will visit the Herr Kruger now.'

He bowed and strode away springily. Kinross became aware of the Australian woman at his elbow.

'Mary,' he said, 'did you hear him? But let me tell you, we can get back to your world, although it will be dangerous. I'll work on it and let you know.'

She seemed hardly to listen, staring after the retreating figure.

'Bonzer!' she cried. 'There walks a man.'

*

Kinross walked away, slightly irritated. Garcia was talking to a group of Latins including the three women. Kinross sought out the Rhodesian, a stocky, florid man wearing plaid shorts. His name was Peter White.

'What do you think of all this?' he asked.

'You have quite a good thing here,' the man replied. 'Like being a child again, isn't it rather?'

Kinross grunted and asked him what he thought of Lankenau. White said he admired von Lankenau, that he had felt rather forlorn and drifting until he had joined von Lankenau's group. Kinross fidgeted over commonplaces for a few minutes and finally said, 'You know, White, we can go back through that gate if we work it right.'

'I wouldn't want to, just yet,' White said soberly. 'This is rather a lark.'

'But in time — when you get tired —'

'Tired? That's as may be. You know, Kinross, the last I remember of the old world was being almost dead of fever in the low veldt. Dreams ... visions ... I'm not ready to wake back...'

'Then you think this is a dream?'

'Yes. A different and a better one.'

Kinross excused himself and walked away shaking his head. Garcia was still yapping in Spanish. He walked aimlessly for a while, then lay under a breadfruit tree near the fire and tried to sleep. He felt bored and angry. He saw two newcomers, both women, come down the hillside and left it to Garcia to welcome them.

*

Hours later von Lankenau strode back from the grove with an exalted look on his lean face. He called his group together and instructed them in their several languages as to their duties. Each must gather a token handful of fruit or berries every morning and place it on the cairn before the cave entrance. Then he spoke of huts and sanitary arrangements. White had a belt axe. One of the Mozambique Negroes had a bush knife and the other a grubbing hoe. When the work was going forward to his satisfaction he joined Kinross under the breadfruit tree. Garcia came with him.

'I talked to the Herr Kruger a long time,' von Lankenau said, sitting down and clasping his long arms around his knees. 'He told me much, and much of it about you, Mr Kinross.'

'What about me?' Kinross asked, narrowing his eyes.

'The special relation between you. Something about the reciprocal way you and he came into this world. He does not understand it himself. But he knows that you should be his lieutenant among the people.'

Kinross said nothing. Von Lankenau regarded him gravely for a moment and continued, 'I will cheerfully defer to your authority, Mr Kinross, and help in any way I can.'

'I don't want authority or responsibility,' Kinross said. 'You go right on taking charge of things, Mr Lankenau, only leave me out of it.'

'If I must, by your default, then I will. But I hope that I can consult with you.'

'Oh, by all means,' Kinross said. 'I'm good at talking.'

'Let us talk then. Do you know, Mr Kinross, this situation is absolutely fascinating. Cannot you feel it set fire to your thoughts?'

'I know what you mean, I suppose. We're tampering with some of the ultimate mysteries. I won't deny I haven't thought about them in my time and read strange books, too. But now I wonder...'

'No moral qualms now, please, Mr Kinross. You will only torment yourself uselessly like that unfortunate Portuguese. We have a world to build and it need not be a copy of the old one. We may be able to simplify the chemistry, systematize the mineralogy ... does not the thought *intrigue* you, Mr Kinross?'

'Huh! You can't beat the energy laws, Mr Lankenau. The more people come in, the more closely they will apply. Kruger told me that himself, and I can see them taking hold already.'

'The Herr Kruger has never worshipped the Second Law. Otherwise none of us would be here. And most of the people who come in will not remain persons, you know.'

Von Lankenau turned a doubtful look on Garcia and continued, 'That is another fascinating thing, to watch the personality elements filter back into external nature until the boundary between subject and object is almost lost. Think of what a power of mass suggestibility we will dispose of then! The very trees and rocks will be amenable to suggestion, each with its indwelling fragment of the human spirit! Oh, Kinross ... your Second Law ... your dry, word-smothered world ... this will be a world of magic for long ages before it becomes a world of science.'

Kinross frowned. 'What right have we to disintegrate personalities in that way? Or to let it happen? Fay and Bo Bo —'

'Those two are special cases, sacrificed to an emergency that will not occur again. As for the others, we will devise a set of ritual life patterns that will stabilize them at some lower limit. That is what I and the Herr Kruger talked longest about.'

'Let me jump into this,' Garcia growled. 'Do you birds think that's going to happen to me? Suppose I won't come apart for you, what then?'

'You may not be able to help it, Mr Garcia. And perhaps you will be much happier when you do ... come apart.'

'You sound like Kruger. Kinross, what does he mean?'

'He means the emptiness of this world pulls you apart, like it or not. Like when you put a lump of salt in a cup of fresh water, it will dissolve a little at a time.'

'Emptiness? Not in the old world?'

'Only rarely, in places like the Antarctic, on a life raft at sea, empty places.'

'I see. Like in most places the old world is already so salty it can't take more?'

'That's the idea. The lumps of salt gain instead of losing.'

'Hmmm. Like we talked this morning. We used to push our devils off on each other.'

'Devils. That is the Herr Kruger's analogy,' von Lankenau interrupted.

'Funny how I know just what he meant by it, without being able to say it any different,' Garcia said.

'You have to lose a few devils before you know,' Kinross told him.

'Well, I've lost some, okay. But I'm still Joe Garcia and my insides work.'

'Name-magic is one of the oldest and most powerful means of binding one's devils into a unity, Mr Garcia,' von Lankenau assured him. 'We will stabilize the villagers well above the name level, I hope.'

'Why do you and Kinross just take it for granted that you're not in line for this ... this devil-losing?'

'We are. We lose devils cheerfully, but it is a selective losing. I, and I suspect Mr Kinross also, we hold ourselves together under a higher magic.'

'It's like this, Garcia,' Kinross said, 'you can either just plain *be* all your devils, or you can be yourself and carry a spare load of devils around with you.'

'Devils, Mr Garcia,' von Lankenau said gravely, 'are bits of experience, large or small, gay or mournful.'

'The lived experiences, good or bad, we bind into ourselves,' Kinross said. 'The unlived experiences, the regrets, the might-have-beens, the just-escaped things, we carry around on our backs. But we *know* it.'

'We're really explaining to each other, aren't we, Mr Kinross?'

said von Lankenau. 'We lose the devils which ride us and we keep the ones which power us. The villagers must lose both kinds indiscriminately.'

'I'm still with you,' Garcia said. 'Keep talking.'

'To draw on your earlier analogy, Mr Kinross,' von Lankenau said, 'might I say that devils exert an osmotic pressure? It is strongly outward on mountaintops and in such places I have shrugged off a thousand devils. But in Berlin or Paris ... back they came in tens of thousands.'

'That I savvy,' Garcia said. 'It's the difference between being on a long cruise and coming ashore for a month. I get a burn on me to ship out.'

'I think you're okay, Garcia,' Kinross said. 'If you weren't, you would've already drifted off like Kerbeck.'

'Is not Kerbeck magnificent?' von Lankenau asked. 'The end product of devil dispersion, an elemental force, with powers we hardly dare guess at. The Bo Bo thing, too, black and savage. Mr Kinross, we pay a price for mind. But we must not let it happen to our villagers.'

'No, I guess not,' Kinross agreed. 'You spoke of rituals...'

'Yes, a pattern of group rituals to take them through their days and nights, perhaps later through seasons. We will keep them in a mass, maintain a local concentration of devils by mutual re-enforcement or successive recapture ... I don't know quite how to phrase it.'

'I see. The thought disturbs me, Mr Lankenau.'

'It need not. I find it exhilarating. I hope that you and Mr Garcia will help.' Von Lankenau stood up and looked towards the hut-building activity.

'We'll think about it,' Kinross said, getting up himself.

'I'll do what I can,' the Mexican said. Lankenau excused himself and Kinross went over to the villagers.

'Kinross, something tells me you're still packing a devil as big as the *Queen Mary*, for all of your brains,' Garcia said.

Krugertown, as they called it, was built in a day. Mary had a large hut of wattle and daub, near the stone-banked communal fire and a little apart from the village cluster, which lay nearer to the dark grove and the cave entrance. Kinross and Garcia built themselves a similar shelter a short way downstream from the fire. Von Lankenau lived in the village. Every morning Kinross and Garcia took a few bananas or a breadfruit to the cairn. Afterwards Garcia often helped von Lankenau with the villagers, but Kinross walked apart with mixed feelings. He climbed about the hillsides, heedless of the growing number of black things and grey women that lurked there. Sometimes he saw Kerbeck, endlessly pursuing the dwarfs and the smoke women, and tried to talk to him. He tried to tell Kerbeck what Kruger had done to him in taking away his humanity. The massive Swede buzzed and hummed and Kinross did not know how much he understood.

Mary walked apart too, always in a flutter of birds. He saw dainty green-and-blue sunbirds, green-and-white pittas, green-and-bronze drongos and the demure white nutmeg pigeons she loved most of all. When they met he tried to talk to her and found her aloof and remote.

'This world is harmful to you, Mary,' he urged one day. 'It disintegrates you, makes you lose part of yourself. Don't you want to go back to Queensland while you still can? Before it's too late?'

'I send out my birds and I call them back,' she replied. 'No harm here.'

'That's no answer, Mary,' he protested. He looked at her untroubled face with the red lips and the smooth brow and laid his arm across her shoulders. She slipped away from him.

'Mary, I'm going to take you back to Queensland,' Kinross said sharply. 'It's my duty to you.'

She hummed like Kerbeck and moved away. Kinross looked after her morosely. Shortly after, he saw her high on the hillside talking to Kerbeck ... Or humming with him.

*

New arrivals came in almost daily, by ones and twos, and melted at once into the village pattern. One day Kinross asked von Lankenau how long he thought it would go on.

'The rate is dropping off,' von Lankenau said. 'I expect it will decrease asymptotically and never quite stop. But the gate apparently sweeps a quite narrow path and has already caught up most of the susceptibles. And it may be that, as this world fills, its power of attraction lessens also.'

'When will it be full?'

'Never, I hope. We want thousands, a large gene pool, a larger world. I estimate our surface is only about five miles in diameter now, Mr Kinross.'

'Can't Kruger make it larger if he likes?'

'Only at the expense of internal definition. He is striking a workable balance. But it is boundless by re-entry, and is not that a most fascinating experience, Mr Kinross?'

'I found it disturbing and then frustrating,' Kinross said.

'Ah! The limits, of course. But with more people we can extend our surface to more comfortable limits. In the end, I suppose, we shall make it spherical and remove the re-entry barrier to a higher dimension. But I shall be just a bit sorry when we do. Do you take my feeling, Mr Kinross?'

'Just who are "we"?' Kinross asked with a sudden edge in his voice. 'You and Kruger?'

'Oh no. All of us. The culture, the Herr Kruger ... you will have a part.'

'You are kind, Mr Lankenau.'

The tall man looked at him sharply. 'Mr Kinross,' he said solemnly, 'any time that you wish to, you may take your rightful position in this world. I urge you to do so. I command by your default, and you know that very well.'

'I'll have no part of it,' Kinross said. 'Damn Kruger and his world, snatching up a young woman like Mary Chadwick...'

'The Herr Kruger loves you, Mr Kinross. You and Mr Garcia are his sensorium, due to the peculiar circumstances of your coming here. He can be aware of his world only indifferently through the rest of us and through the Kabeiroi on the hillside.'

'Well, I don't love the Herr Kruger. I hope he's still mad with thirst.'

Von Lankenau raised a cautionary hand. 'He does still suffer from thirst,' he said in a low voice, 'but your words are unworthy of you, Mr Kinross. Hate me, if you must, but not the Herr Kruger.'

'Why in hell do you have to shave every day?' Kinross asked angrily as he turned away.

He looked back from a distance and tugged at his beard. Mary Chadwick was talking to von Lankenau, standing close, looking up at him. Kinross reflected with a twinge that she had never looked up at him in that way. Then he remembered that she was as tall as himself and could not. He walked away swallowing a curse.

*

That night in their hut Kinross suggested to Garcia that next day they try to break the re-entry barrier. The Mexican declined, saying that he and von Lankenau were working out a path-marking ritual with the villagers.

'Well, I will,' Kinross said. 'I'll go up there and walk right through it by not believing it's there, just like I should have done in the boat.'

'Yes, and got your throat cut,' Garcia said. 'But it's there, all right. You'll find out.'

Kinross found out. He fought the barrier all day, knowing its impossibility, striving to locate the exact point of reversal in order to step boldly across it. He came near doing so. Again and again, with the tiny instant of vertigo almost upon him, he saw the leering Kabeiroi drift by him and birds fly over, but each time he was turned back, suddenly half a mile down the hill and headed the wrong way. He came back home in the evening disgruntled and exhausted.

'Lankenau called it a world of magic,' he reflected. 'Well, magic, then. Birds fly through the barrier. I'm doing this for Mary. If she would only help me —'

He decided to try again during the next thunderstorm, when he hoped Kruger would be too busy with his storm devils to guard the barrier. One morning several days later the sky darkened and the queer light lay along the ground and he knew a storm was making. The black things from the hillside invaded the valley in gusts of damp wind, sidling and eddying through the shrubbery just out of eye reach. Poised on rocks, treetops and all pointed things, the grey women strained upward in a tension of half-visible air. With the first drops of rain Kinross set off up the hillside.

As he neared the barrier zone, the storm grew more violent. Thunder boomed and roared at him, rain slashed at him in sheets, jagged lightning flashes gave him glimpses of the storm devils. The Kabeiroi scurried around him with obscene menaces;

over his head the grey women streamed by on the gusty wind. Once he saw Kerbeck, head thrown back, great chest bared to the wind.

All day he fought the barrier, spitting curses into the storm, and all day the storm spat and thundered back at him. He fell and rolled and rose again, over and over, straining up the hill with aching chest. Wind-driven twigs and branches lashed his face and body. Smothering rain drilled at him; wind snatched his breath away. At last his pounding heart and trembling knees convinced him that he was beaten. He turned back down the hillside.

'Well, Kruger, I gave you a fight,' he gasped aloud. The storm abated as he limped down the slope and he saw downed trees and scattered branches and raw-earth gullies swirling with runoff. The thought came to him that he had at least forced Kruger to wreck von Lankenau's precious village. Then he was on the valley floor and the storm cleared entirely. Half a mile away he could see the village and its trees seemingly intact.

As he neared his hut, Mary came from behind a screen of shrubbery. White nutmeg pigeons perched on her head and shoulders. She smiled at him oddly.

'Regular cockeye bob up there, wasn't it, Allan?'

He looked at her stupidly. 'Didn't it rain down here?' he asked.

'Only a sprinkle,' she said, smiling. 'Go in by the fire and dry your things. You look tired.'

He walked on, soaked, mud-stained, limping on a wrenched ankle. 'She smiled and called me Allan,' he thought. 'No storm here. Called me Allan. Oh, hell . . .'

*

One morning, remote from the village, Kinross heard a pounding noise. In a clearing he found Peter White and two others beating mulberry bark with rounded paddles. The bearded Rhodesian looked tanned and fit and merry-eyed. The three men avoided looking at Kinross, as all the villagers tended to do, but they were aware of him and the rhythm of their pounding faltered.

On impulse Kinross called out. 'White! Come over here!'

White paid no attention. Kinross spoke more sharply. White,

without looking around, mumbled something about the Herr Kruger.

'I command you by the power of Kruger!' Kinross shouted in sudden anger. 'Come over here!'

Reluctantly the man came to the clearing's edge. He looked down, but did not seem afraid. The Bantu and the Kanaka continued pounding.

'White, you were a man once,' Kinross said. 'How would you like to be a man again?'

'I am a man, Mr Kinross,' White said soberly.

'A man needs a wife. Do you have a wife, White?'

'Soon the Herr Kruger will give me one.'

'I mean back home. Do you have a wife there?'

'There is no woman in my hut, but soon the Herr Kruger—'

'Damn your hut. I mean where you came from, in Rhodesia.'

'I have always been here.'

'No, you have not. You came from another world and if you try you can remember it. Can't you, now?'

The man looked up. 'Yes, but I was a lot of different me's then. It was not a good world.'

'Remember it. I command you to remember it by the power of Kruger. Remember your wife and your children.'

The man twisted his body and his face darkened. 'There were many wives and children. It was an underground world. Everyone lived in tunnels that ran in straight lines. They were tumbled together like straws and sometimes they crossed, but none ran side by side. One of my tunnels came through into Krugerworld. I crawled up out of the ground and here I am. That is all I can remember.'

'Okay, go back to your work,' Kinross said.

White did not move. 'First you must lift the name of the Herr Kruger from me,' he said.

'All right, I remove the name,' Kinross said.

'Once more. Twice you placed it on me.'

'Okay, once more I remove it,' Kinross snapped. 'Go on, now.'

He walked away. Behind him a third club took up the pounding and the rhythm steadied.

*

Alone in his hut he raged instead of sleeping. A magic world

... what magic, then? Kruger's teachings ... before the word, before the thought ... what act would serve him now? What blind, wordless, unthinking act?

He decided he would refuse to place his usual token of fruit on the cairn in the morning and suddenly he could sleep.

*

Kinross rose early and walked through the various fruit groves, eating as he walked, until his hunger was stayed. His aimless walking had led him to the edge of the dark timber grove screening the cave mouth. On impulse he walked through the grove into the clearing and on the way discovered with surprise that he had a small guava in his pocket. He threw it away. Two villagers, a man and a woman, were placing fruit on the cairn. Kinross wondered whether they were mated.

Silva, as always, sat beside the cairn. Kinross tried to talk to the old man, patting him on the shoulder, but Silva repulsed him with an incoherent wailing about devils. Kinross shrugged and went back down the valley.

It was beautiful early in the day with birds and flowers colour-spotting the green through which the clean-limbed, scantily clad villagers moved in twos and threes. Smoke rose above clean, red flame before Mary's hut. The air was perfumed with flowers, musical with birdcalls and spiced with woodsmoke. Kinross tried to feel good, but a restlessness drove him.

He walked back and forth, jerkily, sat down and got up again, driven to random action that he would not shape into the action demanded of him. He picked fruit and threw it away, drifted towards the dark grove and walked resolutely away from it. At last he decided to make the fight in his hut. He went inside and wove burrawang fronds into a barrier across the door.

For hours, pacing or lying prone with clenched fists in the gloom, Kinross strove with his rebellious muscles and reproachful viscera. Finally the familiar silvery voice, long unheard, spoke to him out of the air.

'Kinross, I am hungry and thirsty. Bring me fruit.'

'No. You have it from a hundred others.'

'I need it from you, Kinross. We have a relation. I gave you back a lost life. You dragged my body here with your own strength. You owe me a duty.'

'I deny it. If I ever did, I repudiate it.'

'I have power, Kinross. Silva and Kerbeck bring no fruit. Would you be as they?'

'You lie, Kruger. You have not even the lesser power to command my muscles.'

'I don't wish to command them directly. I wish to command you with your consent, in this one small thing.'

'No. I have tested your power before now.'

'Not to the full, Kinross. Not to the full. I have been reluctant to hurt you.'

Silence extended itself into Kinross's abrupt awareness that the tension was gone. He felt as tired as he had on the days he had fought the re-entry barrier. He lay back to rest.

'Round one is mine,' he thought comfortably.

Distant thunder rumbled. 'Round two?' he thought uneasily and unbarred his door. Black clouds were boiling up over the great ridge above the cave mouth. Black storm devils sifted down from the hillsides and grey women danced singly and in groups on the tops of things. Kinross brought wood into his hut, also stones to bank a fire and a brand to kindle it, working rapidly.

The storm built up fast, with tremendous thunder and jagged bolts of lightning. Kinross shielded and tended his fire, unheeding. The drumming rain changed into a drizzle and set in cold. The day became night without a perceptible sunset. Kinross shivered through the long night, burrowed under sweet grass and with his belly pressed against the warm rocks that banked his fire.

Morning was cold and clear. Frost rimed the grass, flower petals drooped and tree leaves twinkled with silver. Kinross was standing in his hut door, shivering and stamping his feet, when he heard the frosty crunch of footsteps. It was von Lankenau, not yet shaven for the day.

*

'Good morning, Mr Kinross,' Von Lankenau greeted him. 'Please pardon my more or less forced intrusion on your privacy.'

'That's all right. It's not an intrusion.'

'Oh? I had thought that you were deliberately keeping to

yourself these last weeks. But I would like to discuss this cold...'

'If you can't take it, grow a beard like me.'

'I am inured to cold, Mr Kinross. At the moment I entered this world I had been stopped on a ledge at sixteen thousand feet for about thirty hours. My arms and my legs were frozen. The Seeings had begun ... you touch my pride, Mr Kinross, excuse me.'

Kinross said nothing.

'How long are you prepared to go on with this defiance of the Herr Kruger?' von Lankenau asked.

'Maybe till hell freezes over.' Kinross laughed harshly, adding, 'No. Until Kruger agrees to let me through the re-entry barrier. Me and Mary Chadwick.'

'He will never let you go, Mr Kinross. And Miss Chadwick does not wish to go.'

'The thing this damned Krugerworld has made of her may not so wish. But if Kruger would give her back to herself—'

'She has never ceased to be herself, Mr Kinross. We talk increasingly of late and I know her well, in time will know her better still. But I do know what you mean...'

'Skip what I mean. Did Kruger send you here?'

'Oh no. It is my curiosity, I am afraid. You interest me, Mr Kinross, and in studying you I learn much about the Herr Kruger. Tell me: you know the villagers are suffering from cold and will soon be hungry: do you feel any responsibility for their sufferings?'

'No. Kruger's responsible. Let him ease off.'

'He will not, I am sure. What then?'

'Then we shiver and we starve. When those lobotomies of yours in the village get desperate enough maybe they'll help me break through the re-entry barrier and get their minds and their own world back.'

'They will not. That I know. But let me congratulate you on your efforts to break the barrier, Mr Kinross. Did you know that you had pushed it outward a good way and permanently distorted that corner of Krugerworld? You are a strong and resolute man, sir. I wish you would consent to take your rightful position among us.'

'I'll take my rightful departure or die trying.'

'Mr Kinross, the villagers also have a right to live. I will not prompt them nor will Mr Garcia. We have agreed on that. But if the Herr Kruger can reach them directly through dreams and inspired counsels, and if the collective will moves to act upon you, we will stand aside also.'

'Fair enough,' Kinross grunted.

'One other thing, Mr Kinross. I fear you may be moving blindly towards a treason of the light. I will say no more.'

Kinross did not answer. Von Lankenau half smiled and saluted him, then turned and left in silence. Within a minute other footsteps approached, light and rapid ones.

It was Mary Chadwick and she was in a fury. Her shirt was half unbuttoned and she clasped in her bosom a dozen or more of the white nutmeg pigeons with black wing and tail tips.

'Down with ice on their poor wings. Half frozen. You stringybark jojo—' she stormed, face twisted with pity and anger.

'I'm sorry—' Kinross began.

'Then stop it, you fool! Stop it at once! Take that silly fruit to that stupid altar and put an end to this nonsense!'

'Did Lankenau or Kruger put you up to this?'

She stared a scornful denial. Kinross swallowed and felt his face burn under his beard.

'Why blame me and not Kruger?'

'Because I can't come at the Herr Kruger and I can come at you, of course. Hop, now!'

'All right,' Kinross said. 'I'll do it for you, Mary. Will you understand that I do it for you and not for Kruger, Mary? Will you accept?' He took hold of her hand among the rustling pigeons and looked into her blue-violet eyes murky with waning anger.

'Of course for me,' she said. 'That's what I came to tell you, idiot.'

'Glory!' Kinross gasped and walked away rapidly. When he came back through the grove the frost had already melted under a warming sun.

'Round two is at least a draw,' he thought, 'but I kind of think I won it too.'

*

Weeks passed into months and the land smiled. Kinross left fruit at the cairn each morning, whispering under his breath, 'For you, Mary.' Also each morning he laid flowers on a quartz boulder he had carried up from the creek and placed by Mary's hut. The flowers always disappeared, although he never saw her take them.

Stragglers continued coming into Krugerworld by ones or twos every few days and the population of Krugertown approached three hundred. Kinross talked amicably with Garcia and von Lankenau from time to time. Von Lankenau discussed the expansion of Krugerworld with an increasing population. He thought that at some critical point it would expand enough to accommodate another village and perhaps be dumbbell-shaped rather than elliptical. Garcia told Kinross pridefully that Pilar was carrying a child, he hoped a son.

Sometimes Kinross talked with the villagers. They had lost all memory of their origin. They believed they had come from underground, shaped of earth's substance at the bottom of a great pit, and that sometime they might go back there to sleep again. They had no clear notion of death.

Kinross no longer wandered aimlessly. At a site a mile down-valley from the village, he built a stone hut. He built it massively, bedding large stones from the creek in clay and rammed earth, giving it several rooms beamed with ironwood and heavily thatched with nipa fronds. He built a stone fireplace and crude furniture.

Mary passed by several times a day, taking little interest in his work. When the house was complete she would not come in to look at it.

'It is a waste of strength and good living time,' she said, laughing. 'Allan, Allan, walk under the trees again.'

'Will you walk with me?' he asked.

She laughed and turned away.

Kinross built a walled garden around the hut. He brought water into it with a raised ditch, pierced for drainage, taking off from above a low dam he built in the creek. It fed a bathing pool and turned a small waterwheel. He threshed out grass seeds and spread them and berries on the flagstones of his garden. Birds came and ate, but Mary would not come in.

'You don't paddock me with anything cold as stone, not by half,' she said.

He saw her more often with von Lankenau and gradually tended to avoid them both, nagged by a question he dared not ask for fear of an answer. The black moods came back and he neglected his house to roam the hillsides as of old. Sometimes he met Kerbeck, vacant-eyed and enormous, wild and shaggy as a bear, and cursed Kruger bitterly while Kerbeck buzzed and hummed. He did not fail to leave his token of fruit each morning on the cairn.

Then one day, leaving Kerbeck and the Kabeiroi on the hillside, he came into the valley and saw a village woman tending grapevines alone at the foot of the hill. She was young, supple and brown and wore only a short paperbark skirt. She stopped working and bowed her head, waiting for him to pass. He stopped and searched in his mind for his limited Spanish.

'*Cómo te llamas?*'

'*Milagros, señor.*' Her voice was very low and she would not look at him.

'*Bueno. Tu estás muy bonita, Milagros.*'

'*Por favor, tengo que trabajar ... el Señor Kruger ...*'

'*Ven conmigo, Milagros. Yo te mando por el nombre del Señor Kruger.*'

She flushed darkly, then paled. She looked up at him with beseeching eyes shiny with tears.

'*Por favor, por gran favor, no me mande usted ...*'

'*Quién te manda?*' asked a new voice from behind the screen of vines, and then, 'Oh. You, Kinross?'

Garcia came into view around the vines. Like Kinross, he was barefooted and wore only stagged-off dungaree trousers.

'What's it all about?' he asked.

'I was trying to talk to her.'

Garcia spoke rapidly in Spanish and the woman answered in a fearful voice. The thickset Mexican turned back to Kinross, fists knuckling hipbones.

'Take the name of Kruger back off of her, Kinross!'

'I remove the name, Milagros,' Kinross said. 'Garcia, I—'

'Take it off in Spanish,' Garcia interrupted. 'You put it on in Spanish.'

Kinross garbled out a sentence in Spanish. Garcia was still angry. He sent the woman away.

'Kinross, I can't take away your power to use the name of Kruger. But if you use it wrong, I can beat you half to death. Maybe all the way to death. You get me?'

'Don't judge me so damned offhand. How do you know what I intended?'

'Milagros knew. She knew, all right. I believe her.'

'Believe what you like, then.'

'Listen, Kinross, stay away from the villagers. I command you in the name of Garcia and his two fists. You can out-talk me and out-think me, but—' The stocky Mexican struck his right fist into his left biceps with a solid thump.

Kinross clenched his teeth and breathed deeply through flaring nostrils. Then he said, 'Okay, Garcia. I appreciate your position. The only man I really want to fight doesn't have a body.'

'Good,' the Mexican said. 'No hard feelings, then. But you still stay clear of the villagers, a kind of agreement between you and me. Okay?'

'Okay,' Kinross said and walked away.

When he came into his walled garden he saw nutmeg pigeons pecking at overripe mangoes he had placed there for them. Fearless, they hardly made way for his suddenly slowed feet. The two fluttered briefly when he, unthinking, bent and seized them. They quieted in his hands and he carried them inside, wondering why.

For hours after nightfall he sat before his fire and stared into the red coals. So he could out-think and out-talk Garcia, could he? Well, yes, he could. But the act? How get at a man without a body?

Where was Kruger vulnerable? What force could he align against Kruger? He had touched Kruger once only, and that was by a refusal to act. That was negative. Now what was the positive side? What act, what unthinking, nameless act ... and

the fit stole over him and he took up the pigeons and left the
house and walked through the dark grove to the cairn where
Silva moaned in sleep and did what there was to do and returned
and slept, to wake unremembering.

*

Day was advanced when Kinross came out of his house. He
walked up the valley, crossing over the little stream to avoid the
village, and picked two overripe mangoes, which he carried
through the grove to the cairn. Silva was rocking and wailing
thinly in an extremity of woe. To the right a knot of silent
villagers clustered.

On the cairn he saw the headless pigeon with blood-dabbled
feathers and the black, sticky blood on the stones. Fingers
tugged at his memory and he frowned, refusing to think what
this strange thing might mean. He flung down his mangoes
into the blood spots with force enough to burst them and said
aloud, 'For you, Mary.' Then he stared arrogantly at the knot
of villagers and strode away. But he was reluctant to emerge
from the grove, prowling its tangled shades far from path and
stream for upwards of an hour. Then he walked back towards
the village.

A strange silence held in the land. No air moved. The villagers
were drifting towards the grove in small groups, without the
customary singing and talking. He heard no birdcalls. Then,
as he neared the village, he heard a woman's voice strident
with grief and anger. It was Mary.

'What kind of Kelly rules do you keep here, you and your
Kruger, you smooth-faced blood drinker?'

Then von Lankenau's voice, soothing and indistinct behind
the huts, and then Mary again, agonized, 'Oh, my lovely white
sea pigeons! Poor dears, poor dears, I'll take them all away
with me. You'll pay! You'll pay!'

She broke into a loud humming and came into view, running
towards the hillside. Her long hair streamed behind her and
her once lovely face was frightfully twisted and gaping with
menace. Kinross noticed with another start that the black
grotesques from the hillside had invaded the valley floor and
were all about the village. They gave way before the infuriated

153

woman and all at once the birds became vocal, deafeningly so, clouds of them swooping at the black things with squawks and screeches.

Kinross stood in vagueness, looking around. Never had he seen the sun of Krugerworld more warm and smiling, the flowers more voluptuous, the trees more heavily laden with bright fruit. At his feet earth tilted and crumbled and a red-capped mushroom emerged, visibly rising and unfolding. Von Lankenau, his shaven face set in grave lines, came towards Kinross from out of the cluster of huts. Before he could speak, Garcia shouted from the direction of the grove and they saw him running towards them.

'Something's haywire with the villagers,' he told von Lankenau, panting. 'They won't follow ritual. They won't obey me.'

'What are they doing?' von Lankenau asked.

'Nothing. Just standing still. But I don't like the feeling of things in there, don't ask me why.'

'Something of truly enormous significance has happened, Joe. I do not know what ... I was about to ask Mr Kinross for his ideas. Those pigeons ... but you are right, we must get the villagers back to their huts and to the fruit groves. Perhaps Mr Kinross will help us.'

'How do you know I won't play Pied Piper and lead them clear out of Krugerworld?' Kinross asked, his thoughts beginning to mesh again.

'Perhaps, now, that would be merciful. I truly do not know, Mr Kinross. But let us see what may be done.'

A distant scream came out of the dark grove, repeated, a volley of screams.

'Silva's voice!' Garcia exclaimed. '*Por Dios*, what now?'

He started running back towards the grove. Kinross and von Lankenau ran after him. The screaming ceased abruptly.

In the clearing, villagers stood in silent groups on either side of the stone platform and in small groups elsewhere. On the cairn lay the body of the old Portygee, looking fragile and collapsed. His head was crushed horribly.

Garcia swore softly in Spanish. Von Lankenau said musingly, 'Now, for as long as Krugerworld shall last ... I must manage to understand, I must!' A dark memory itched in Kinross's fingers.

'Kinross,' came a whisper from close behind their heads. The men whirled as one, to see nothing.

The whisper continued, still behind their heads so that they whirled again, vainly. 'Thank you, Kinross, for teaching me how to relieve my thirst. My terrible thirst. I will purge my world of thirst, Kinross, with your service.'

Von Lankenau gripped Kinross's arm with iron fingers. 'What have you done, Kinross?' he pleaded. 'Tell me. I must know. *What have you done?*'

'You'll never know,' Kinross said harshly. 'Look behind us.'

The three men turned round again. The villagers had compacted into a mob with a concave front that was slowly closing in on them. Von Lankenau ordered them back in whiplash tones, to no effect. He turned to Kinross, his face pale and grim.

'Command them under the name of the Herr Kruger, if you can, Mr Kinross. We have no other chance.'

'Stop, damn you, in the name of Kruger!' Kinross shouted. His hands were sweating and his heart was in his throat.

They did not stop. The horns of the crescent met on the far side of the cairn. The solid front of the villagers, coming on in a slow amoeboid shuffle of hundreds of feet, was ten yards away. Kinross saw the girl Milagros, teeth bared. They had seconds only before, as Kinross somehow knew, they would join Silva on the bloody stones.

'Quickly, Kinross,' von Lankenau said. 'Tell me while there is time. *What have you done?*'

'Heart's truth,' Kinross whispered, 'I don't know. *I don't know!*'

'Let's give 'em a fight,' Garcia growled, then, 'Hey! They've stopped!'

A cloud of birds came over the clearing, flashing in many colours, circling and shrieking. Brush crackled and water splashed in the dark grove. Then something went wrong at the back of the mob of villagers. It shuddered and broke into fragments which crept rapidly to either side, opening an aisle through its midst.

It was Kerbeck, floating hair and beard ablaze with sunlight. Rags of clothing fluttered on the great, bronzed limbs. Sweeps of his massive arms knocked villagers a dozen feet through the air. Booming and buzzing, wide blue eyes two-dimensional and unknowing, he passed the three wonder-stricken men. In his wake ran Mary Chadwick, birds about her head.

'He's going in to kill Kruger's body,' she told them, coming to a halt. The frightful malevolence still rode in her features and Kinross's fear was not wholly relieved.

'*Madre de Dios!*' Garcia gasped.

They watched the giant Swede round the stone platform and head for the cave. From the darkness floated a gobbling howl that sent a hair-bristling shudder down Kinross's back. The great form of Bo Bo emerged to block the entrance.

Kerbeck ran forward with a shout. The Negro ran to meet him with his bubbling squall. The two massive figures shocked together and the world seemed to tremble. They swayed, stumbling back and forth, locked in furious embrace, and a great sighing moan went up from the fragmented mob of villagers. Kinross felt a hand on his arm and glimpsed von Lankenau's white, rapt face beside him.

Black giant with white strove and roared and howled and stumbled. They cannoned into the cairn and destroyed it, scattering and treading the stones underfoot like pebbles. They splashed into the creek and out of it, broiling the clear water to dark turbidity. Both giants were increasing in stature, to Kinross's eyes, clearly superhuman now. The force of their roaring and howling beat down on him with physical pressure. He saw Mary Chadwick on his right, blue-violent fire blazing in her eyes, fierce red lips parted eagerly.

First one giant and then the other was forced to his knees, only to rise again in thunderous shouting and howling. The fight drifted nearer to the cave mouth, entered and swirled out again, entered and stayed. Kerbeck's hair and beard seemed to shine with a light of their own, dwindling sparklike into the depths. The gigantic battle shouts became a continuous hollow roaring under the earth. Kinross felt a hand shaking him insistently. It was von Lankenau.

'Go now,' he was saying. 'For certain, the barrier will be down momentarily. I begin to understand. I almost – I do salute you, Mr Kinross. Take the woman, if she will go.'

Kinross collected his thoughts. 'Mary, will you go?' he asked.

'Too bloody right I will,' she said, 'and take my birds off with me!'

Kinross looked at Garcia and held out his hand. 'Part friends, Joe?' he asked.

'I don't savvy this, Kinross,' the Mexican said, 'but good luck and get out of here.'

Kinross shook hands with the two men. Then he and Mary Chadwick, arms linked, walked rapidly back towards the village.

*

The dark grove swarmed with Kabeiroi, but no more than a scattering of the ugly shapes could be seen on the open valley floor. The sky was overcast and the diffuse, watery light of the early days lay again on the valley. The old indefinite quality was back, nothing quite in full view.

'Mary,' Kinross said. 'I do believe we're already through the barrier. Space has drawn in around the cave mouth.'

'Good-oh!'

Kinross led her up the hillside, talking feverishly. They would marry, he said. He was quite well off, had a good job doing confidential work for the US government. He had lots of back pay coming for his last job and a bonus, too, when he told them about it. They would live in California, it was a lot like Queensland. Trips, the theatre, music, a fine home, gracious living.

Mary said little. Birds kept fluttering in to land on her head and shoulders but the number around her did not seem to increase. The light grew weaker as they climbed and the land more indefinite. When they reached the height of land and Kinross knew for sure that they had escaped, it was almost dark. From time to time a rippling quiver ran over the ground sending them sprawling, but they rose and pressed onward. As before, progress seemed timeless and effortless. There was no moon.

Mary lagged behind him and Kinross kept turning to wait for her. By degrees in the fading light he saw the strained malevolence of her expression give way to a vague and remote sorrow. The wide brow was smooth again, red lips dreaming. Once she said, 'My birds. I can't get back all my birds.'

Suddenly the wailing cry of a stone curlew reached down from the darkness. Mary stopped and looked up. Kinross turned back to watch. The forlorn, throbbing cry repeated. Mary raised her arms to the black sky and crooned. Nothing happened.

She looked at Kinross, both of them vague in shadow. 'It won't come down to me,' she whispered plaintively.

A third time the call floated downwards. Mary dropped her arms.

'I'm going back,' she said. 'You go alone, Allan.'

'No!' he protested. 'You must come with me. I won't let you go back!'

He seized her shoulders. She came stiffly erect and a light gleamed from her eyes. A touch, a twinge only, of the old feeling hit him and his knees turned to water. He collapsed, kneeling, clasping her around the thighs, pleading, 'No, no, Mary! Don't leave me alone here in the dark!'

'I must,' she said calmly. Then with a touch of pity, 'Be brave and go along now, Allan. It is all you can do.'

She raised him and kissed his forehead. He stumbled away, not daring to look back for fear of a renewed weakness. The sky rifted with silver as the overcast broke up and presently a full moon rode high ahead. He looked back then, but she was nowhere.

On to the great pit under the moon, leg over leg unthinking. It was all he could do now. He found the ravine and waded down it, outrunning the current. He heard the roar of falling water and saw the last rock shoulder that interposed itself between him and the brink. For just a heartbeat he clung to the rock and stared into the pit with all its silver beauty and its reflecting pool in the bottom. Then, not letting the water take him only, but rushing, pitching his body forward, he went over the edge.

It was not a sheer drop but, rather, a series of stages. Plunge and strike and roll, plunge and strike and roll, rhythmically, painlessly, with intolerable excitement of the spirit, down and down he went until the circle of sky above him smalled with distance and the silvery pool below waxed enormous. It was as if the great pit were reversing its dimensions, flexing through itself, turning inside out, as if he were falling into the moon. Then, on the very point of an unbearable instant, the waters closed over him.

Down, down through the water, pain and darkness and fear vice-clamping his chest, kicking and waving his arms and there was a dry crackling and a pain in his toe and he sat in the thorn scrub gasping. His skin was dry.

It was daylight. A stream ran nearby and above it reared a yellowish sandstone ledge with figures of paunchy kangaroos and stick men done in faded red and black. He picked up a handful of earth and looked at it. There it was, hard and sharp and clear in all of its minute particulars, deep as any microscope might probe, solidly there beyond all tampering forever. It was the old world. His world. Kinross stood up, feeling an overpowering thirst.

He went down to the creek and drank deeply and was as thirsty as before. He buried his face in the water and drank until he was near bursting and rose, wavering on his feet, thirst tearing at him unbearably. He tugged at his beard and wondered.

Sounds came, a jingle of metal and splashing. Then the creak of leather and low voices. Riders were coming up the creek. Suddenly he sensed them directly, horses and men, radiant with life, red, living blood pumping through veins and arteries. His thirst became a cloud of madness enfolding him, and he knew who and what he was.

He waited, wondering if they would be able to see him ...

The Swarm 60p
Arthur Herzog

A family of five on a country outing are attacked by bees – Mr and Mrs William Peterson die as a result of bee stings. Their three children are also attacked.

This was the beginning, barely noticed. Only a few scientists felt the first stirrings of terror. But then the death toll began to mount – and terror erupted into national panic as great swarms of savage bees, deadly killers, blotted out the sun as they spread across America ...

The Man Who Fell to Earth 60p
Walter Tevis

Who was this tall, abnormally thin stranger who called himself Newton? Why did he need half a billion dollars immediately? What was the secret behind Newton's revolutionary inventions? Was there a master plan conceived in another part of the Solar System? Must Newton be destroyed by jealousy, mistrust and suspicion, or can he save two worlds from destruction – Earth and his own planet?

David Bowie stars in Nicolas Roeg's film of *The Man Who Fell to Earth*, a successful British Lion release.

You can buy these and other Pan books from booksellers and newsagents; or direct from the following address:
Pan Books, Cavaye Place, London SW10 9PG
Send purchase price plus 15p for the first book and 5p for each additional book, to allow for postage and packing

While every effort is made to keep prices low, it is sometimes necessary to increase prices at short notice. Pan Books reserve the right to show on covers new retail prices which may differ from those advertised in the text or elsewhere